The Tangled Web

DAYBREAK MYSTERY

B·J·HOFF

Accent Books™ is an imprint of David C. Cook Publishing Co.
David C. Cook Publishing Co., Elgin, Illinois 60120
David C. Cook Publishing Co., Weston, Ontario
Nova Distribution Ltd., Newton Abbot, England

THE TANGLED WEB

Cover design by Koechel/Peterson & Associates, Inc.

First Printing, 1988
Printed in the United States of America
96 95 94 93 92 7 6 5 4 3

Library of Congress Catalog Card Number 87-70365
ISBN 0-78140-475-4

FOR JIM

Husbands are the real heroes . . .

In Appreciation

To Roger Mast—
For being so patient with a "city girl."

To Gary Kauffman—
For all kinds of "technical assistance."

And to Jo Ann Moser—
"Plot Knot Spotter" extraordinaire

Thanks, guys!

Like a father who untangles
What small, clumsy hands ensnare,
God unsnarls and smooths our problems
Once we trust them to His care.

B.J. Hoff
From *The Weaver*

Prologue

Pittsburgh, Pennsylvania *Saturday*

Teddy felt the sick force of emotional pain in the pit of his stomach as he walked to the massive mahogany desk in the library. Nick's body was slumped over it. His boss, his teacher, his surrogate big brother. He had been shot execution style, murdered by someone he had once called a friend. One of the *Family.*

Teddy shuddered, forcing down the rancid taste of his own terror as he touched Nick's lifeless shoulder, then felt for a pulse at the side of his neck. His worst fears confirmed, he yanked his trembling hand away. He wondered if Nick had suffered and had to quickly squeeze his eyes shut against the hot tears that threatened to spill over at the thought.

Finally, he opened his eyes and scanned the extravagantly decorated room with a sweeping glance.

Heavy, rust-colored drapes were closed against the late afternoon gloom. The room was dim, lighted only by a hand-painted desk lamp.

The telephone receiver was off the hook and growling with demand. Teddy started to pick it up, then stopped. *You want your fingerprints on that, jerk?*

He glanced down and saw the open top drawer of the desk. He knew it had been forced. Nick always locked the top drawer on the left. Always. That was where he kept his gun. And where he had once kept the small notebook.

He bent over, peering into the drawer but not touching it. Both the gun and the notebook were gone.

Teddy expected the notebook to be gone. Nick had told him where it would be hidden. *But what about the gun?*

He wiped both hands on his jeans, then raked his fingers through his dark, curly hair in a gesture of anxiety. For an instant, his shock at finding Nick dead was replaced by an unexpectedly powerful wave of grief. The man slumped over the desk had been good to him, had trusted him, confided in him, advised him.

"Stay out of the business, Teddy," Nick had often warned him. "It's not for you. You're a good kid. You shouldn't sell yourself out. Just work for me, personally. Not the Family."

Nick Angelini was the only man Teddy had ever trusted. Nick had become his family, he and the kids.

The kids!

His head snapped up sharply. *Where were the kids?*

His boots whacked the glistening wood floor as he bolted from the library. He stopped in the hall, squinting up the dark stairway.

"Nicky?" His voice echoed in the high-ceilinged entrance hall. "Stacey? You up there?"

As he stood there, unmoving, his mind replayed his earlier conversation with Nick. At the time, he hadn't realized it would be their *last* conversation.

"They're going to hit me, Teddy. At least, they're going to try. I violated the *omerta,* the code of honor. They know about the notebook, that I'm going to turn it in and testify against Sabas." His dark eyes had raked Teddy's face, studying him closely. "I hate to do this to you, *compagno.* But I've got no one else. You know where I've hidden it. Now you have to take the notebook and the kids, Teddy."

They were standing in the garage, and Teddy started to back away from Nick, shaking his head, holding up both hands palm outward. "Uh-uh. No way. I'm a driver, a gofer, not a hero."

"You're more than that, and you know it," Nick said with soft rebuke. "You are like *fratello mio*—my brother. You love my kids. And they love you. If they lose me, they have nobody. A dead mother they don't even remember, a dead father—"

"Your sister—"

"—is a stranger to them. You're family."

"No one's going to hit you, Nick," Teddy continued to protest. "Get out. Take the kids and leave."

"Teddy, Teddy," the older man said, shaking his head sadly, "you know better. I've betrayed the Family. There's nowhere to run. Nowhere."

"Nick, I can't do what you're asking," Teddy insisted in a rush of words. "I'm not like you, Nick. I'm not tough, I'm not even brave. I drive cars, Nick. That's all. I can't take care of your kids, man. I have nothing to offer them. Besides, you're talking crazy. How could anyone know about the notebook, about what you're planning to do?"

Unexpectedly, the older man's face settled into the granite mask usually reserved for another mob leader. "Sabas is going to have me killed," he grated roughly, grabbing the front of Teddy's jacket. "The word is out. I'm a dead man. And you know as well as I do what will happen to my kids. They'll be raised by one of the other *caporegimes*. I don't want that for my kids, Teddy! I want them to grow up clean and decent, not caught in the web of the business."

Abruptly, he dropped his hand away and slapped Teddy lightly, affectionately on the cheek. "Sorry, kid. I'm nervous today, that's all."

"What do you want me to do?" Teddy didn't even try to mask his resentment. He owed Nick. But this much?

"I want you to take the kids and the notebook and get out of here," Nick said eagerly. "Before tonight. I have money for you—a lot. Enough to take care of the three of you for a long time if necessary. But you've got to go *now,* as soon as possible!"

"But *where,* Nick?"

"To a place in Virginia. There's a man there who'll take care of you and the kids. You can trust him. He works for the Federal Witness Program," Nick explained hurriedly. "He's been straight with me. Once you get the notebook to him, they can move on Sabas, put him out of business. For good. Everything they need is in that notebook, Teddy. Even without my testimony, they can finish him."

Nick's eyes were shadowed by hopeless resignation when he added, softly, "I'll never testify, Teddy. It'll never happen. But you can save the evidence. And you can save my kids, if you'll do what I ask. Will you, Teddy?"

They studied each other for a long, silent moment. Then Teddy nodded shortly. "I'll need a car. My 'Vette is still down. There's no time to finish it."

"Take the limo."

"It's low on fuel. I was planning on going into town later this evening and filling it up."

"Do it now. I'll have Nora pack for the kids while you're gone."

"Nora's off today, remember?" Teddy felt a pang of sympathy for the kindhearted, elderly housekeeper who adored both Angelini children. She would grieve for days when she realized they were gone.

"Then Nicky can pack for both of them."

"You're coming with us, or I'm not going."

"*No!* The only chance you and the kids have is to go without me. If I go, they'll get all of us. You and the kids have to go alone." He paused. "Maybe I can buy you a little more time by staying here."

He then took Teddy into the library and gave him a bundle of money from the safe, more money than Teddy had ever seen. "Now get moving," Nick ordered. "I'll talk to the kids while you're gone. They'll be ready when you come back."

Still Teddy had hesitated. "Nick . . ."

The older man had swallowed hard, then reached out to grip Teddy's shoulder. "Thank you, *compagno*. You've been a good friend."

Some friend, Teddy now thought with self-disgust as he called the kids' names once again. *I've let Nick be murdered and lost his kids, all within two hours.*

He bounded up the stairs, taking them two at a time. Calling the children's names, he raced down the carpeted hallway to Stacey's room. He threw open the door, stopping just inside the pink and gold bedroom. It was empty.

Next he went to the boy's room, but Nicky, too, was gone.

He started down the hall, flinging open one door after another as he went. After checking the entire second floor and finding nothing, he ran back downstairs, charging through each enormous, drafty room with mounting anxiety.

Had they taken the kids?

In desperation, he hurtled down the basement steps. He crossed the concrete floor, stopping beside the dark gray furnace. His eyes narrowed at a sound somewhere above his head.

"Nicky? Stacey? Are you down here?"

A soft thump coming from overhead, a few feet away, made him look up. Quietly he began to move in the direction of the sound.

"Stacey? Nicky? Can you hear me? It's Teddy."

He was answered by a faint whimper. Not moving, he looked up at the laundry chute. Slowly, he raised both hands to unlatch the hook on the wooden drop-bottom, holding it so it wouldn't fall open. He stepped to one side and cautiously opened the chute.

Stacey tumbled out first, practically falling into Teddy's arms. He tucked the ebony haired, sobbing little girl securely against his chest with one hand, then reached up to help her brother.

Nicky landed lightly on his feet and stood staring at Teddy, his dark eyes burning with a combination of fear and anger behind thick-lensed, silver-framed glasses.

"What are you guys doing in the *laundry chute?*" Teddy snapped incredulously.

The chunky little girl in his arms began to cry in earnest, and he immediately gentled his tone, patting her helplessly on the back. "Don't cry, baby. It's all right." He gave one stubby pigtail a gentle tug. "Look at Mrs. Whispers," he said, pointing to the none-too-clean rag doll Stacey was clutching tightly to her heart. "She isn't crying."

He turned to the boy. "Are you kids okay?"

With the back of his hand, Nicky brushed a tangle of dark, ragged hair away from his forehead and asked bluntly, "He's dead, isn't he?"

Teddy stared at him without answering, still cradling the sobbing little girl against his shoulder. He glanced at Stacey, then nodded shortly to the boy.

"Where were you? Did you see anything?"

Nicky swallowed, his thin neck making the reflex motion appear strangely pathetic to Teddy. "No. Papa sent us upstairs. He told us to hide if we heard anyone in the house."

Removing his glasses, the boy wiped his eyes with a weary gesture, much as an older person might have done, then replaced them on the bridge of his nose. "Someone kept banging on the door." His voice wavered for an instant, then he lifted his chin and said evenly, "It was quiet for a few minutes. Then we heard a shot."

Teddy moistened his lips and glanced from Nicky to the weeping little girl in his arms. He wished he could think of something to say. He wished he could *think*.

"Papa said you were going to take us somewhere," the boy went on in an odd, flat tone of voice. "He told me to pack a suitcase for both of us. Are we still going to leave?"

Teddy nodded. "Yeah. Right now. You've got your stuff ready?"

"It's in the kitchen."

"Let's go." Still holding Stacey in his arms, Teddy turned and started up the basement stairs.

When they reached the hallway, he glanced toward the open library door.

The boy started toward the room.

"Don't go in there, Nicky!" Teddy cautioned sharply. "Get your coats, both of you. We have to get out of here."

Nicky looked at him, then at the open door, hesitating.

"Don't, Nicky," Teddy said tersely. "You don't want to go in there."

The boy continued to stare toward the library for another moment, then turned, crossed the hall, and opened the closet door.

Murmuring softly to reassure Stacey, Teddy gently set her to her feet and took her hand. "Come on, baby. Let's get you into your coat."

Teddy zipped up his own sleek racing jacket, then helped Stacey into her red parka. "That's my good girl," he said softly, managing a smile as he straightened.

She was no longer crying, but her dark brown eyes were large and solemn. "Nicky said we can't see Papa anymore, that he isn't going with us." Her small voice sounded frightened and much younger than her six years. "Mrs. Whispers is going with us, isn't she?"

"Anywhere you go, Mrs. Whispers goes, sweetheart," Teddy assured her with a hug.

In the kitchen, Teddy looked out the window, then cracked the connecting door to the garage, peering out the opening.

A thought struck him, and he twisted his mouth to one side impatiently. "You kids wait here a minute. I have to make a quick call before we go."

He returned to the library, resolutely averting his eyes from Nick's body. His hand shook as he dug a handkerchief out of his back pocket and used it to pick up the receiver. He pressed the button to clear the line and get a dial tone, then called Frank Vincent, Nick's lawyer.

A natural mimic, he changed his voice and hurriedly advised Vincent of Nick's murder. He then fled the room, not looking back.

In the kitchen, he picked up Stacey's suitcase, started to open the door to the garage, then stopped. He turned to Nicky. "There's a notebook," he said. "One of those little pocket jobs. It was important to your papa. Do you know anything about—"

Before he could finish, Nicky nodded. "Papa told me. It's safe."

Teddy heaved a sigh of relief. At least Nick's death wasn't entirely a waste. "Get your stuff and come on," he said, gesturing toward Nicky's suitcase and wishing he'd had time to pack a few things for himself.

Teddy hurried them into the garage, fumbling for his keys as he went. Now if only they could get out of here without being seen. Maybe they had a chance.

"Where are we going?" Nicky wanted to know, lifting his suitcase into the silver limousine's large trunk.

Without answering, Teddy hustled both children into the front seat, then ran around the car and got in on the driver's side. Before activating the automatic garage door opener, he punched the key into the ignition, pressed the power lock to secure the doors, and waited only a few seconds for the powerful engine to roar to life.

As soon as the door went up, he backed out of the garage, tires squealing.

"Where are we going, Teddy?" the boy asked again.

Teddy righted the limo, glancing in the rearview mirror as the car surged forward. "On a long trip," he finally said. "I'm taking you to a place your papa told me about."

Without looking at him, Nicky replied knowingly, "Where we'll be safe."

Teddy glanced over at him. "Where you'll be safe," he repeated. "That's my job now," he said softly. "Keeping you and Stacey safe."

"You can't get away from them, you know," Nicky said woodenly. "There isn't anywhere we can go that they won't find us."

Teddy knew that Nicky was one smart kid. A genius, the supervisor at that fancy private school had told Nick. An honest-to-goodness nine-year-old genius. At the moment, however, Teddy fervently hoped the kid wasn't so smart he couldn't occasionally be wrong.

1

East Central West Virginia *Palm Sunday*

Jennifer came awake in an instant, bolting upright in bed, alert to something wrong. Apprehensively, she pulled the blanket up to her neck and tried to focus her eyes in the dark bedroom.

The room was thickly shadowed, unfamiliar. It was also cold. She looked toward the blue iron bedstead at her feet, then across the room at the wall-to-wall sliding glass doors.

Outside, it was dark, a dense, threatening darkness. Huge pine trees and gnarled, grasping maples fought each other for control of the night sky. The blackness was relieved only by a faint spray of golden-pink from the security light that stood a few feet away from the cabin.

The cabin.

Gradually, her head began to clear. They were at the Farm, not at home. She glanced over at her husband. Daniel was still asleep, his breathing deep and regular. Jennifer squinted at the digital clock on the bedside table. It was almost midnight.

She had been asleep for over an hour, exhausted from the ride to the Farm and all the lifting and tugging she had done after they arrived. They had carried in supplies from the Cherokee and wood for the fireplace, then stocked the pantry shelves. At eleven o'clock, Jennifer had collapsed gratefully onto the plump feather bed, every muscle in her body rioting in rebellion.

She was fully awake now, though, as she tried to figure out what had awakened her. There had been a noise—a noise that didn't belong. Keeping the covers wrapped snugly around her shoulders, she listened to the silence of the cabin.

Suddenly, a soft thumping sound, like the muffled thud of running feet, broke the quiet. At the same time, Sunny, Daniel's golden retriever guide dog, stood and uttered a low, warning growl from her place on the other side of the bed.

Someone was on the deck.

A wraparound wooden deck rimmed the cabin with steps descending to the yard on both sides. It sounded to Jennifer as if someone was at the other end of the cabin, the side on which the kitchen was located.

Abruptly, the sound was gone. Once again there was only silence, a silence so total that Jennifer could hear her own heart pounding. She stared with rising dread at the glass doors at the end of the room, half-expecting to see someone stop in front of them and gape back at her.

Giving one more perfunctory growl, Sunny went to stand in front of the doors and look out. Staring straight ahead, Jennifer stretched a trembling hand to tug at Daniel's shoulder.

"Daniel. Daniel, wake up." She had meant to whisper. Instead, fear roughened her voice, and her words scraped the hushed bedroom like sandpaper.

Immediately alert to the alarm in Jennifer's tone, the retriever came to stand at her side of the bed.

"Um?" Daniel was slow to stir. "What?"

"Daniel, I heard something." This time Jennifer was able to manage a clear whisper. "On the deck."

"Mm."

"*Daniel!*" She shook him hard. "There's someone outside!"

Gripping his shoulder, Jennifer hunched rigidly under the

blankets, waiting for some sign of life from him, all the while keeping her uneasy gaze fastened on the sliding glass doors.

Finally, Daniel made an intelligible sound and pushed himself up. "What's wrong?"

"I heard something outside," she whispered hoarsely. "It sounded like someone running across the deck."

Realizing that Daniel was awake, Sunny left Jennifer and went to the other side of the bed. The retriever stood, patiently watching as her master shook his head with a groggy frown and an enormous yawn.

"Running, you say?"

Jennifer flipped back the blankets and swung her feet over the side of the bed. "I'm going to see what's going on," she said, grabbing her robe from a nearby rocking chair and hurriedly slipping into it.

"Jennifer, wait a minute—" Daniel reached for her, but she was already creeping stealthily across the plank floor, flinching at the cold wood beneath her bare feet.

"I want to be sure those glass doors are locked," she whispered over her shoulder.

There were no drapes at the doors, a situation Jennifer intended to remedy before sleeping another night in this room. She would use sheets or blankets or anything she could find, she decided.

Edging cautiously up to the side of the glass, she took a deep breath, then peered outside. Seeing nothing, she forced herself to walk in front of the doors and check the lock. It was secure.

Quickly, she turned and went to the window at the side of the room, opening a shutter so she could look outside.

Although Daniel could see nothing—he had been blind for nearly six years—he shrugged into his robe and made his way to the window, coming to stand behind her. Sunny followed him, pressing between the two of them.

"Can you see anything?" Daniel murmured, resting one large hand on her shoulder.

"Nothing." Jennifer strained for a better look, but her view was obscured by the dense grove of trees that enfolded the cabin. There was nothing to see but darkness and waving shadows.

Daniel touched her face. "How long have you been awake?"

"Just a few minutes. The noise woke me up."

"You don't suppose Jason is up wandering around, do you?"

Jason was their nine-year-old son, adopted from the County Children's Home a few months earlier. He was mildly retarded, and Jennifer had to continually fight her impulse to over-protect him. At the moment, he was supposed to be sleeping in the loft bedroom.

She turned to look at Daniel. "I didn't even think of that! We'd better go see if he's still in bed," she said, turning away from the window.

"Wait—I'll go with you."

"Do you want Sunny's harness?"

"No, I know my way around the cabin well enough. She can just follow us." He waited for Jennifer to place her hand on his forearm before starting out of the room.

"I wonder if Gabe or Lyss heard anything," she whispered as they left the bedroom.

Lyss, Daniel's sister, had married Gabe Denton in January. Gabe was not only Daniel's best friend but was also assistant manager and program director of the Christian radio station Daniel owned and managed in Shepherd Valley. The newlyweds had come along this week to help prepare Helping Hand Farm for its first visitors of the year.

Weekend campers would begin to arrive the week after Easter.

For the last four years, Daniel and Gabe, as well as others from their church, had worked to convert what had once been a family-owned farm into a Christian summer camp for handicapped children. This year, the two couples had offered to give the overworked, year-round supervisor and his wife an opportunity to take a brief vacation before the summer camping season.

"If Gabe wakes up, we're *all* up for the night," Daniel muttered as they made their way through the darkened great room to the loft stairs. "The man responds to two hours sleep the way most normal people feel after ten. He'll yak till dawn if he gets up now."

Jennifer left him and Sunny at the bottom of the stairs while she went up to check on Jason. The boy was sound asleep in the enormous old four-poster that had once belonged to Daniel's grandparents. She pulled up the quilt he had kicked off, then went back downstairs.

"It couldn't have been Jason," she whispered to Daniel when she returned. "I don't think he's moved since we tucked him in."

She looked at him, then suggested uncertainly, "Daniel, maybe you *should* wake Gabe and have him look around."

"No way," he said at once, louder than he had intended. "It was probably just a wild dog, Jennifer. Let's go back to bed." He turned to leave the room.

"A *wild dog?*" Jennifer repeated incredulously, grasping his arm to stop him.

He nodded. "We get them all the time out here. People dump them on the highway, and they come looking for food."

Jennifer blanched at the thought of wild dogs circling the

cabin, then felt her stomach knot even more when she remembered the noise she had heard. "That was no dog," she said stubbornly. "Not unless he was wearing shoes."

Daniel sighed and rubbed one hand down the side of his thick, black beard. "Whatever you heard, darlin'," he said reasonably, "is gone now. Come on—let's get some sleep." He covered her hand on his arm, starting hopefully toward the bedroom.

He moved a little too fast for Jennifer, however, and she crashed into the corner of a large pine table, stubbing her toe hard. Unable to stop herself, she collided with Daniel's back, yelping with surprised pain.

"Ohhh, Daniel . . . ohhh . . . my *toe!*"

Daniel quickly put one arm around her waist, clasping her shoulder with his other hand to steady her. Sunny stood quietly watching, occasionally uttering a soft whimper of curiosity.

"What's wrong, honey? What'd you do?"

"My toe," she wailed. "I think I broke my toe!"

"How'd you do that?"

She looked up at him, then snapped with exasperation, "I ran into a table! It's pitch black in here."

He seemed to consider her words as he patted her back in a comforting gesture. "Why?"

"Why *what?*" Her eyes smarted with tears from the pain.

"Why is it dark in here? Why didn't you turn on the lights?"

She continued to stare at him blankly, saying nothing.

He grinned at her. "Just because I navigate pretty well in the dark, darlin'," he drawled, "doesn't mean you have to."

Light suddenly shot through the spacious room causing Jennifer to jump. Gabe, startling in a Chinese red monk's robe trimmed in gold satin, stood there staring at them. Directly behind him, peering over his shoulder with sleepy eyes, was Lyss. She looked lost and somewhat forlorn in a bathrobe that strangely resembled a too-large horse blanket.

Gabe studied them, his hand still poised on the light switch. "What's happening?" he grumbled, flipping a shock of sun-streaked blond hair out of his eyes. "What are you guys doing out here in the dark?"

"We were looking for a wild dog wearing shoes," Daniel said mildly. "But Jennifer—who apparently *isn't* wearing shoes—stubbed her toe. Will one of you take a look at it?"

Gabe studied his friend's expression for a moment, raking his index finger across his dark mustache. Finally, he shrugged and walked over to Jennifer. Carefully, he helped her to a well-worn but comfortable looking chintz chair by the immense stone fireplace, steadying her as she sat down.

Lyss watched them vacantly, yawning and running a hand through her dark, tousled hair. After a moment, she moved, slowly, going over to Jennifer and kneeling down to look at her foot.

"I don't think it's broken, Jennifer," she said after examining the toe through glazed eyes. "It's not swollen or anything."

"Well, it *feels* broken," Jennifer said defensively.

Lyss turned to look up at Gabe, who rolled his eyes and shrugged again.

"So what's going on?" he asked for the second time. "Why are the two of you wandering around in the dark? It's after midnight."

Daniel explained while Lyss went to make an ice pack for Jennifer's toe.

"Probably a 'coon," Gabe said wisely after Daniel had finished. "Or maybe a wild dog."

Jennifer gritted her teeth. "I don't want to hear any more tonight about wild dogs, if you don't mind."

Daniel suppressed a grin and insisted Jennifer go to bed with the ice pack as soon as Lyss came back with it.

Jennifer noticed that he quickly discouraged Gabe's offer to make coffee for everyone—"as long as we're all awake anyway."

"Some of us," Lyss told her husband with a bleary-eyed glare, "are *not* awake. Nor do some of us *want* to be awake. Certainly not for the next eight hours."

Within minutes, the cabin was again dark and quiet. Daniel was almost asleep when Jennifer whispered beside him, "I *did* hear something, Daniel. And whatever I heard, it wasn't a dog."

The bearded, stoop-shouldered driver hunched behind the wheel of the dark limousine glanced nervously at the man on the passenger's side of the front seat. He started to speak, stopped, cleared his throat and tried again.

"How much longer are we gonna keep looking, Wolf?" His voice was reedy, almost whining.

The smaller man looked at him, his pale blue eyes frigid. He studied the driver for a moment, then, without answering the question, turned his gaze back to the road. Pressing his index finger to one side of his nose, he sniffed, once, then again. The gesture appeared to be involuntary, an old habit.

In the back seat, a thick-set man with thinning hair and a heavy mustache stirred and woke with a grumble as the car slowed, then came to a stop.

"Where are we?" he slurred irritably. "Why are you stoppin', Boone?" Chuck Arno wiped a meaty hand across his eyes, forcing himself awake. He stretched, then leaned forward on the seat far enough to look at himself in the rearview mirror. He grimaced at his reflection, that of an overweight middle-aged man with oily skin and dark eyes, now red-rimmed and bloodshot. Automatically, his mind snapped shut, denying what he saw. He looked away.

"Got to get some gas," the driver snapped. "Hard to tell where we'll find another station this late out here in the sticks."

The wiry man with the odd blue eyes finally spoke. "Give the Boss a quick call when you find one. He'll be wondering what's going on."

"You call, Wolf," wheedled the driver. "You know he's gonna be mad."

Wolf looked at him. "Why would P.J. be mad, Boone?" he asked blandly.

Boone killed the engine but continued to stare straight ahead. His large, somewhat gnarled hands were none too steady on the steering wheel.

From the back seat, Arno watched the driver squirm, mildly amused at his discomfort. It was a standard joke among the other mob soldiers that Boone Scavarelli spent half of his life being scared to death of the Boss—P.J. Sabas—and the other half shaking in his shoes because he was terrified of Wolf.

Arno felt a familiar sting of impatience with Boone when he glanced back at him, as if looking for support. The older man's cast eye was an imperfection that grated on him. He could never quite tell where Boone was looking. In addition, Arno thought with distaste, the tall, too-thin man was grizzled, bumbling, and none too bright. For the life of him, he couldn't figure why Wolf insisted on taking old Boone along wherever they went.

The aging driver was still pleading with Wolf. "He'll likely think we should have caught up with them by now."

"P.J.'s a patient man," Wolf answered with another sniff. "Just tell him we're closing in."

"Closing in?" Boone looked at him incredulously.

Wolf smiled at him. In the back seat, Arno moistened his lips, fidgeting as he studied the man in front of him.

Jay Wolf was neither ugly nor attractive. At first glance, he might have been labeled nondescript, with his fair, acne-scarred complexion, his small, narrow-shouldered frame, and his limp, light brown hair. But when he smiled, his otherwise innocuous appearance underwent a striking transformation. His lips opened on a wide mouth that was overcrowded with surprisingly large teeth, some of which tapered to fang-like points. At the same time, his pale eyes narrowed menacingly, making his surname, "Wolf," eerily appropriate.

Still smiling broadly, he nodded. "That's what I said, Boone. Closing in."

"But, Wolf, we ain't got a thought where they—"

The smile disappeared. "Here's how I see it, Boone," he said, casually resting one arm against the car door. "We've temporarily lost Giordano and the kids, true. But if we cover every county road, every country lane, and every cow path, we'll eventually find them. Right?"

He paused, again smiling as if he'd magnanimously forgiven the older man his temporary lapse of confidence. "Now, Boone, you know they can't hide a flashy silver limousine like Angelini's out here in the woods too long. It looks pretty simple to me. We find the car, we find Giordano and the kids. Even if they try to hole up somewhere, they can't ditch that limo without us finding it, eventually. Isn't that what you think, Chuck?" He turned to look at Arno.

Caught off guard, Arno hesitated, then gushed, "Right, Wolf. That's how it looks to me."

Wolf nodded and turned around. "You see, Boone? Just tell the Boss we're closing in and things are looking good. Real good."

Without meeting his gaze, Boone pulled up the zipper of his hooded jacket and hauled himself awkwardly out of the car. He pumped his own gas, paid the attendant at the register inside, then lumbered over to the pay phone at the side of the stucco building.

"Boone's nervous," Wolf said conversationally, his eyes on the older man using the phone. "You nervous, too, Chuck?"

"Me?" Arno laughed a little too loudly. "No way, Wolf. Nothing to be nervous about, right? It's like you said. How hard can it be to spot that limo of Nick's?"

A cold finger seemed to touch the back of his neck when Wolf half-turned and smiled at him. "Boone's getting old, I'm afraid. We'll have to watch him, Chuck."

Arno quickly agreed. "Yeah, maybe we'd better."

Wolf was still smiling when Boone returned to the car. "So, did you talk to the Boss?"

Boone nodded brusquely, giving Wolf an anxious look. "He's burnin'. Just like I said."

Wolf shrugged. "He'll be okay. Relax, Boone. You worry too much." He touched his nose and sniffed. "Let's move."

Boone started the car and eased away from the pump, glancing uneasily at the man next to him. "He's really upset, Wolf. You know what he said?"

"No, Boone. What did he say?" Wolf asked with exaggerated patience, smoothing the velvet lapel of his gray Chesterfield.

"He said to tell you to bring Giordano and the kids back by the end of the week or we'd better not come back at all. He said that, Wolf."

The younger man looked at him for a moment, then turned away, saying nothing.

In the back, Arno folded his arms across his chest and slouched down in the seat. Sometimes he wished he was still collecting markers. At least then he wouldn't have to spend so much time with Wolf. The guy gave him the creeps, and that was the truth. There was something weird about him, something . . . tainted.

He had never met anyone like Wolf. Even the Boss—who could turn mean as a snake sometimes—wasn't scary like Wolf. At least with P.J. you always knew where you stood; you could tell when you were in trouble with him.

But not the Wolf. The guy was totally unpredictable. Icy cold most of the time, except when he had one of those fits of his. Then he turned into a crazy man, a real mental case. And you never knew when it was going to happen. He would be smiling that blood-freezing smile of his one minute, and the next thing you knew, he'd be roaring and crashing around like a rabid . . . wolf.

Arno shuddered inside his black leather jacket and told himself, not for the first time, that when this was over, he was going to talk to the Boss about some new action. Something out of Wolf's territory.

2

Monday

By dinnertime the next day, Jennifer had decided that her sore toe was a blessing in disguise. Her work detail for the day had been the lightest of all, and now, listening to the others rehash their efforts, she could enjoy the conversation guilt-free.

Her chief duties had been to help Gabe inventory the storage pantry and give him a hand with lunch and dinner.

By mutual consent, Gabe had been appointed chef for the foursome. His hobby was cooking, and he approached it as he did everything else, with dizzying energy and a somewhat awesome degree of creativity.

His menu for the evening meal was no exception, Jennifer thought, dishing up a generous second helping of the Creole gumbo she had watched him concoct earlier.

Lyss was reluctantly studying the last bite of food on her plate. Glancing across the kitchen at her husband, who had already left the table to start scraping dishes, she said soberly, "I guess I'll forgive you for not helping us clean cabins. This is scrumptious stuff, love." She lifted the final taste of gumbo to her mouth with relish.

"Save room for dessert," Gabe cautioned her.

"Dessert, too? What'd you make?" Daniel asked with interest, pushing himself back from the long harvest table and contentedly thumping his abdomen.

"Lemon mousse," Jennifer announced, knowing her husband's fondness for anything citrus. "And almond cookies."

Daniel made a small sound of satisfaction and stretched deeply. "When's snack time?"

Jason soaked up the last bite of gumbo on his plate with a piece of roll and started to put it in his mouth. A glance at the retriever sitting next to him, however, made him stop. He studied the dog's hopeful gaze for a moment. After a furtive glance at the adults, none of whom seemed to be watching, he quickly palmed the roll and started to give it to Sunny.

"Don't even think about it, Jason," Jennifer said warningly, eyeing the boy and the dog.

Jason studied her face. When he saw one corner of her mouth twitch, he grinned at her, knowing he was still on safe ground. Blinking once, he said gravely, "But Sunny hasn't had any dinner."

"Well, she's not going to have her dinner at the table," Jennifer said firmly. "You can feed her after we're done. Outside."

"You'd better not give her any of that gumbo, Jason," Daniel told him. "It's too spicy."

"So spicy you had three helpings," Gabe countered dryly from the sink.

"I'm immune," Daniel said pleasantly. "I'm used to Jennifer's cooking."

Jennifer elbowed him. "Give him gummy oatmeal for breakfast, Gabe. Nice and cold."

Wiping his hands on a dish towel, Gabe left the sink and came back to the table. He scooted onto one of the pine benches across from Daniel. "My count in the storage pantry didn't tally, Dan. Either Mac's first count was wrong, or there's some stuff missing."

"What kind of stuff?" Daniel asked, crossing his arms over his chest and leaning back against the wall.

"Blankets and pillows. I was three short on each. Jennifer checked my count, just to make sure."

"Don't forget the food shelves," Jennifer reminded him. "According to the list Mac gave us," she explained, turning to her husband, "there should be two large jars of peanut butter in addition to what we counted. Plus three bags of marshmallows and two boxes of crackers."

Daniel leaned forward, drained the milk from his glass, then dabbed his mustache with his napkin. He rose from the table. "Mac is as accurate as a CPA with that storage pantry," he said, carrying his dishes over to the sink. "Maybe some things just got misplaced somewhere."

"Nope. We checked every likely place," Gabe replied. His green-eyed gaze swept the room. "Who's up for the dishes tonight?"

When a long silence greeted his question, he sighed and said evenly, "Okay. Who wants to get up at six tomorrow morning and cook breakfast?"

"Jennifer and I will take care of the dishes," Daniel quickly offered, already pushing up his sweater sleeves. "You just sit down and enjoy your coffee."

Gabe smiled at Lyss and Jennifer. "Cooperation. That's what makes this team *work*."

When they were at home in Shepherd Valley, Monday evenings usually found the two couples and Jason at one of the local nursing homes for Bible study and worship. Since that wasn't possible tonight, they all went into the great room after dinner to have what Jason called "Prayer and Share Time."

Jennifer loved this room, mostly, she had once told Daniel, because it was so *friendly*. The huge stone fireplace was the focal point of the entire room, and a fire was burning there anytime the mercury dipped low enough to allow it. Everything in the room was old and well-used. The furniture was big, worn and comfortable. She thought of the cabin as a second home, and this particular room as the heart of that home. It was a happy room, she often thought, a good-natured, smiling kind of room where people could be themselves and enjoy each other.

Gabe had made a fire earlier, and it continued to blaze cheerfully while Daniel retrieved his old Martin flattop guitar from the corner of the room. Lyss went hunting for her banjo, and for over an hour, they sang camp choruses, followed by a time of prayer and sharing together.

Finally, Daniel got up and put his guitar away, saying, "I'm ready for dessert."

"We'll get it," Gabe offered, pulling Lyss up from the couch with him. "It's in hiding. You don't leave dessert within reach of Dan the Dumpster."

When they came back, Gabe was empty-handed and scowling. "Okay, so you found the cookies, Kaine. Are there any left?"

Daniel, standing with his face toward the fire, turned with a puzzled frown. "What?"

"The cookies, Daniel," Gabe repeatead with forced patience. "Where are the cookies?"

Lyss followed her husband into the room, laughing at his aggravation. "Better 'fess up, Dan. He's just stubborn enough to lock up the mousse if you don't share the cookies."

"What are you two talking about? I don't know anything about the cookies."

Jennifer thought Daniel's innocent expression looked entirely genuine, but she could never be sure, not around him and Gabe. "Gabe, you said you made two dozen. Even

Daniel can't eat that many cookies in an afternoon."

They went on arguing another few minutes, Gabe insisting that his brother-in-law was the only conceivable suspect, while Daniel's injured look of denial became more and more convincing.

"I've got it!" Jennifer exclaimed suddenly.

Gabe looked at her, waiting.

"I'll bet it was that wild dog you fellows told me about last night," she said sweetly.

Gabe shot her a disgusted look.

Jason finally ended the exchange. "I bet I know who took the cookies."

All four adults stopped talking and turned to look at him.

From his place on the hearth beside Sunny, he pushed a strand of straight blond hair away from his eyes and said, "Probably it was the children in the woods."

No one said anything for a moment. Finally, Jennifer asked, "What are you talking about, Jason?"

He looked up at her and smiled. "I saw them today, when I took Sunny outside. While Daddy and Aunt Lyss were cleaning the cabin. A boy and a girl. I think they want to be my friends."

"Jason," Daniel said patiently, "didn't we just have a talk a few days ago about make-believe friends? I thought you were going to stop pretending."

Still smiling, the boy shook his head. "But these aren't pretend friends, Daddy. They're real."

Daniel frowned. "Jason—"

As if wounded by the unfamiliar note of irritation in his adopted father's voice, Jason suddenly stopped smiling and fastened his wide brown eyes on Daniel. "They *are* real."

"Jason, *you* didn't take the cookies, did you?" Daniel asked sternly.

"No, sir." The boy's tone and crestfallen expression reflected dismay that Daniel would even ask.

Gabe and Lyss discreetly left the room during the somewhat awkward silence.

After a moment, Jennifer said, "Jason, these . . . children . . . where exactly did you see them?"

"Jennifer!" Dan's tone was sharp.

"Wait, Daniel—please. Let him tell us."

"They came from behind the tree." Jason watched Jennifer's face carefully.

"What tree, honey?" she pressed.

"The big one, at the end of the gate."

"What did they look like?"

He thought for a moment. "The boy has black hair, like Daddy's. And big glasses."

"You said there was a girl, too?" Jennifer prompted him gently, smiling at him.

Jason nodded. "She has tails that stick out like this." He raised both hands to his ears and made a pulling motion.

"Pigtails? Is that what you mean?"

Again, he nodded. "She's little," he said in a condescending tone. "And round."

"Round?" Jennifer repeated.

"Not like you. She's—" he made the shape of a ball with his hands—"round."

"Jennifer, do you really think we should encourage this?" Daniel asked shortly.

Jennifer was surprised at the annoyance etched on his face. She turned back to Jason. "Why don't you go up and get ready for bed, honey?" she quietly suggested. "Maybe we'll talk more about this in the morning. Okay?"

Jason gave her an unexpectedly wise look, as if he knew no one believed him. He rubbed Sunny's ears once more, then got up. "Can Sunny go with me? Just for a while?"

Jennifer nodded. "But she has to come back downstairs in a little bit. Daddy might need her."

As soon as Jason and the retriever were out of the room, Daniel turned his face in Jennifer's direction and said, "You know I've been talking with him about these imaginary playmates."

Jennifer bit her lip and nodded. "Yes, I know. But I'm not sure I understand why it bothers you so much."

"Because he carries it too far sometimes." Shoving his hands into his pockets, he turned away from her, saying nothing more.

Puzzled, Jennifer stared at his broad back. "Daniel? Don't you think you might be making too much of this?"

When he turned back to her, his strong, dark-bearded face was set in a stubborn mask. "No, I don't. But I think *you* could take it a little more seriously."

"Daniel—"

"Jason's different, Jennifer," he said, ignoring her attempt to interrupt. "He doesn't always think about things as you or I do. Sometimes it seems hard for him to tell the difference between what's real and what isn't. I just don't want his fantasies to become too important to him."

Exasperation pushed its way to the surface of Jennifer's feelings, then ebbed as she wondered about her husband's rare touchiness. "Daniel, what's wrong?" she asked hesitantly.

"Wrong?"

"It isn't like you to make an issue of something so small."

He said nothing, but his chin jutted out a fraction more.

The totally irrelevant thought flitted through Jennifer's mind that Daniel suddenly appeared extremely . . . large to her. It wasn't so much his considerable height, nor his incredibly broad shoulders, molded by years of strenuous, disciplined training as a former Olympic gold medal swimming champion.

In fact, Jennifer was seldom mindful of his size. Daniel was so gentle, kind, and tenderhearted that she simply forgot how he towered over her and others. His innate consideration for the feelings of other people, his wonderfully sweet and unfailing devotion to her—even his quiet, casual Appalachian drawl—made it easy to forget that he was still a giant of man, capable of almost formidable strength and power.

Indeed, the only times she ever gave any thought at all to that fact were those extraordinarily rare times when Daniel was being either stubborn—a trait of the Kaine family, Gabe insisted—or angry. Since his bouts of stubbornness were infrequent and brief, she paid them little attention. As for anger—it was an emotion almost foreign to his nature. Only an insult to his God or the abuse of another human being or defenseless animal could incite Daniel to genuine anger.

She decided this was just a stubborn time, so she drew a deep breath, with some confidence, and said evenly, "Daniel, let's take a walk."

He frowned. "A walk?"

"Yes. Would you like to?"

After a moment, he shrugged and replied, "I suppose. But it's cold out."

"I know. I'll get our parkas." She started for the closet, then stopped. "Do you want Sunny?"

"No, if you don't mind helping me."

She looked at him with genuine frustration and said quietly, "You know I don't mind."

She got their coats from the closet and ducked her head

into the kitchen to tell Gabe and Lyss where they were going.

Outside, she tucked her hand under his arm, waiting until he covered her hand with his own before starting to walk.

They went around the front yard, then started down the narrow lane leading away from the side of the cabin. The night was cold, blanketed with damp silence. There was enough wind to bend the low-hanging branches of the maple trees, enough to make the pine trees moan and chant their mournful songs to each other.

Jennifer shivered, as much from the strange sadness hovering over the night as from the cold. She huddled a little closer to Daniel.

"You cold?" he asked her.

"I'll be okay after we walk a bit. I hate to say it, but it feels as if it's going to snow."

He nodded but said nothing.

"Daniel... is something bothering you? Something besides this thing with Jason?" She glanced up at him, feeling a familiar tug at her heart at the strength and kindness molded in his profile.

He didn't answer right away. His voice was soft when he finally said, "It isn't Jason. It's me."

They stopped walking, but she continued to clasp his arm. "What do you mean?"

He sighed. "I don't know. Maybe I'm just overcompensating."

She looked at him, genuinely puzzled. "I don't understand."

"Neither do I." His smile was grim. "All I know is that lately I've been feeling kind of... anxious. Maybe even a little insecure, about being a father." He hesitated. "A *blind* father. To a retarded boy."

Jennifer caught her breath in dismay. "But you're a *wonderful* father to Jason! And he absolutely adores you!"

"Oh, I know he loves me—us," Daniel quickly agreed. "But that's not what I mean. I just want to be sure that I'm doing what's best for him, whatever will help ensure a decent quality of life for him when he grows up." He squeezed her hand. "It's always going to be harder for him, Jennifer, because of the retardation. I want to do everything in my power to give him as much strength and wisdom as he's going to need some day. So he can do more than just . . . survive, if the time ever comes when he's on his own."

Jennifer studied his face, almost strangling on the love welling up in her. "Oh, Daniel . . . don't you realize that Jason can't be anything *but* strong with the kind of love and caring he's going to grow up with?"

She reached up, lightly placed her hands on either side of Daniel's face, searching his sightless blue eyes as if she were trying to look into his heart. "Daniel, you're a *marvelous* father, truly, you are. And Jason is going to grow up to be a fine, strong man, in spite of his handicap." She paused. "But just as your own father didn't try to limit you—even after you were blinded—you mustn't try to limit Jason either."

He rested his hands lightly on her shoulders but said nothing.

"Daniel," she continued, still framing his face with her hands, "you told me once that your father taught you about boundaries by giving you freedom and combining it with responsibility. You said he taught you about right and wrong by letting you make some wrong choices and take the consequences of your mistakes. Remember?"

He nodded, and she went on. "We talked about God often teaching us in the same way, giving us the freedom to stretch and grow by giving us the freedom to sometimes be wrong."

Again he nodded, remembering.

Jennifer dropped her hands away from his face to rest them on his shoulders. "Well, Daniel, I think that's what you have to do with Jason, too. You have to give him some freedom. And," she hesitated, "and I think you have to give him time to be a little boy. That's an important part of growing up, after all."

They continued to stand that way, unmoving, each of them clasping the other's shoulders as Daniel seemed to carefully consider her words. Finally, a hint of a smile softened his features. "And I suppose you think Jason's make-believe friends are a part of growing up, as well?"

"I do. I had a pretend friend when I was a little girl. His name was Bob."

"Bob?"

"He was a big brother type," she explained matter-of-factly. "Protected me from all the bullies on the block, that kind of stuff."

He put his arms around her. "Somehow, kid, I can't imagine you having too much trouble with bullies."

"No?"

"Nope. It's a lot easier to imagine you chasing the bullies away." He kissed her gently on the forehead.

"I did that, too. But only when Bob was with me."

He shook his head knowingly, then lifted his face, listening to the sound of voices drifting toward them from the cabin. "Did Gabe and Lyss come outside, too?"

Jennifer turned to look back at the cabin. "They're on the deck." She smiled as she watched Gabe hold Lyss in his arms. "Acting like newlyweds."

Daniel tightened his embrace, coaxing her closer. Leaning into his strength, Jennifer smiled at how warm it always seemed to be in his arms. She turned her face up to him, catching her breath at the adoring look on his face.

"Do you still feel like a newlywed, Mrs. Kaine?" he asked softly, a smile in his voice.

"As a matter of fact, I do," she whispered, reaching up with one hand to touch his bearded cheek. "Do you, Daniel?"

He pressed his lips into a heavy wave of auburn hair at her temple. "Nope."

Miffed, she tried to pull away from him, but he held her, smiling at her indignation. "I feel," he murmured against her temple, "like a man who is more in love with his wife than any newlywed could ever be." His lips met hers in a gentle kiss. "I love you, Jennifer Kaine. I love you more, right now, at this moment, than I've ever loved you."

"You're sure?"

"Absolutely." He kissed her again, a husbandly kind of kiss that took her breath away.

Then, tucking her arm inside his, he said, "Let's leave the newlyweds out in the cold and go back inside to the fire, what do you say?"

They began to walk. "By the way," he said, stopping, "what did this . . . *Bob* fellow look like?"

"He was gorgeous."

"Thought you were just a kid."

"I was." She smiled. "But Bob wasn't."

He started walking again. "Some day I'm going to have the last word in one of these conversations."

"Wanna bet?"

Someone was crying.

At first Jennifer thought she had been dreaming. Still only half-awake, she reached out to touch Daniel, fumbled for his shoulder, then tapped his pillow. He was gone.

She sat up and looked around, trying to focus her eyes in the darkness. "Daniel?"

When he didn't answer, she reached over to turn on the bedside lamp, then changed her mind.

Again came the faint, muffled cries that sounded like a child weeping, penetrating the night with a chord of anguish.

For a moment, Jennifer couldn't move. Chilled, she clutched the blanket, whispering Daniel's name once more. Finally, she slipped out of bed, fumbling for her robe.

Something must be wrong with Jason.

Trembling now, she pulled on her robe, then stopped, looking toward the window. The sound was coming from outside. But that was impossible. Jason was upstairs.

Hurriedly, she belted her robe and went to the window. Seeing nothing, she turned and went to the sliding glass doors, pulling back an edge of the printed sheet she had hung only that morning to serve as a makeshift drape. The deck and surrounding yard were dark. Nothing moved.

And the crying had stopped.

Rushing across the room and out into the hall, she nearly careened into Daniel who was coming from the great room. Instead of his robe, he was wearing jeans and a ski sweater. Sunny was with him, on her harness.

"Daniel! What's wrong?"

He found her hand and tucked it under his free arm. "I thought I heard something. Did I wake you?"

"You heard it, too!" she exclaimed. "I'm sure I heard a child crying. Is Jason—"

"Jason's sound asleep. That was my first thought, so Sunny and I went up to check on him. He's fine."

"Then what did we hear?"

He shook his head. "Must have been an animal. Maybe something's hurt outside. I'd better go check."

Jennifer threw a coat on over her robe and went with him. They walked around in the cold darkness for nearly half an hour, but found nothing. If an animal *had* been nearby, it was gone. They finally gave up and went back inside.

"At least this time you heard something, too," Jennifer said grudgingly as they hung up their coats. "Do you really think it was an animal?"

"What else?" He unfastened Sunny's harness and stroked the retriever's head for a moment.

"Daniel . . . "

"Hm?"

Jennifer knew what she was thinking was unlikely. Still . . .

"Daniel, what if Jason *did* see someone today? What if those children weren't make-believe?"

He frowned. "In the woods?" He gave a small laugh. "Jennifer, it's *cold* out there. Even a runaway wouldn't be hanging around outside in this kind of weather."

What he said made sense. But *something* had been out there. And Jason had seemed so *certain* about those two children.

"I sure hope the whole week isn't going to be like this," Daniel said wearily.

Jennifer stared at him, only half-aware of what he was saying. "Like this?"

"I'd like to get some sleep."

"Oh." She looked at him, vaguely wishing he felt more like talking. "Daniel . . . *could* someone be out there? In the woods?"

He sighed. "Would *you* be slinking around a youth camp in thirty-degree weather at midnight, Jennifer?" He reached for her hand. "Honey, forget it. Let's get some rest."

She followed him into their bedroom almost reluctantly. In her mind, she could still hear the mournful, heart-wrenching sound of a sobbing child. She knew Daniel was probably right, that it was a ridiculous notion to even think that a child—or an adult, for that matter—would be hovering about in this weather.

But an hour later, she was still awake, listening. Listening for a sound that never came.

3

"Come on, Sunny—this way." Jason darted a glance over his shoulder to make sure the retriever was following him as he took off running toward the immense, gnarled sycamore tree at the end of the lane.

"*Hurry!*" He had to find the children before someone came looking for him. He was sure the children wouldn't come out if they saw a grown-up. He didn't know exactly *how* he knew that, but he knew.

When Daddy agreed to let him take Sunny outside to play, he had warned him to stay "within shouting distance." He wasn't disobeying, he decided, as he and the retriever pounded down the dirt pathway at top speed. He could hear if anyone should call him. The important thing was to find the children and tell them they had to return the cookies.

But what if they had eaten all the cookies by now?

Uncomfortably, he remembered the way everyone had looked at him the night before. Daddy had looked disappointed, and that had hurt a lot. Mommy had looked at him the way she always did, with a little smile that crinkled up her chocolate eyes and made him feel kind of important. Uncle Gabe and Aunt Lyss had just looked as though they felt sorry for him.

He had gone to bed angry, angry with those children in the woods. He was still . . . *gritty*. That was Mommy's word for upset, and that's how he felt this morning.

They shouldn't have taken the cookies. They had no right. That was stealing. Not only had they done something wrong, but what they had done had made Daddy angry with *him*.

"Sunny, stop!" To slow himself down, he grabbed at a low-hanging branch of the big old sycamore tree where he'd been playing the day before. The retriever slowed, then began to prance around the trunk of the tree, running to and from Jason as if she couldn't wait to see what they were going to do next.

"Hey!" He peered into the thickly wooded grove that began in the clearing where he now stood, fanning out across the field and climbing up the side of the hill that overlooked the farm. "Hey, are you in there?"

Sunny looked at him, then turned to stare into the trees as if she, too, were anticipating the appearance of the children.

The only response to Jason's call was the sharp hacking of a nearby crow, followed by a surprisingly strong gust of wind whizzing through the trees.

Disappointed, he dug at the ground with the toe of his sturdy hiking boot, aware that his daddy did the same thing when he was trying to work out a problem in his mind.

Again, he shouted into the trees, somehow knowing as he did that there would be no answer. Still, he waited, unwilling to give up until he heard the sound of his daddy's voice, calling him back to the cabin.

He turned to go, stopping once to look back into the grove with an accusing glance before breaking into a run toward the cabin.

That night, after Mommy had given him the last in a whole series of goodnight kisses and left his bedroom, his daddy stayed, instead of going out with her as he usually did.

Jason looked up with surprise when Daniel sat down on the bed beside him and said, "Jason, I owe you an apology."

He patted the bedclothes in search of Jason's hand and,

finding it, tucked it inside his own much larger one. "About last night," he explained. "I know you well enough to know you wouldn't have taken those cookies. I shouldn't have even felt a need to ask." He paused, then added, "If I hurt your feelings—and I'm afraid I did—I'm sorry."

Jason studied the sightless blue eyes that appeared to be fixed on his face. Even though his daddy couldn't see, he always seemed to be looking at him when they talked, as if what they were discussing was really important.

"I just want you to know I'm sorry, and I believe you when you say you didn't take the cookies. Will you forgive me?"

Jason hadn't seen his daddy look sad very often. He almost always looked happy. Aunt Lyss said he usually looked as if he were about to play a trick on someone.

But right now, he looked sad, and Jason hated that. He sat up in bed and put his arms around his daddy's neck. "It's all right, Daddy. I forgive you."

"I guess we still have a mystery, though, don't we?"

Still hugging him, Jason nodded his head. "You mean, because we don't know who took the cookies?"

"Right. I know what you said, about the . . . children in the woods taking them. But—"

"You still don't believe they're real children, though, do you? You think I made them up."

"Jason, if they seem real to you—"

Jason drew away and looked at him with puzzlement. "Why don't you believe me?"

He saw his daddy take a deep breath. "Jason—" He stopped, ran his hand over his chin, and said again, "Jason, I just don't understand how there could be two children out there in the woods somewhere. It's cold, and there's nowhere they could keep warm. Who do you think these children are? Where did they come from?"

Jason felt a little better. At least he was *trying* to believe him.

"Maybe they ran away from home."

"But they sound awfully little to be doing something like that. How would they get 'way out here?"

"I don't know," Jason said softly, watching his daddy's face. He could see that even though he was trying to believe, he didn't. He would have to find a way to convince Daddy. The apology made him feel good, but he wanted his daddy to *understand*, to believe him. The children were real. He hadn't made them up; he was getting too old for that kind of stuff. He would just have to figure out a way to prove he wasn't imagining them.

He hugged Daniel hard and kised him on the side of his cheek where he always did, on the place where his black beard was thickest. He liked the way it tickled his nose. When he grew up, he was going to have a beard, too.

Long after his daddy had left the room, he lay awake. It was important that he not fall asleep. He had to think, and he always found it easier to think when he was alone.

Tomorrow, when no one was around, he would talk to Uncle Gabe. If anyone could help him figure out a way to catch the children, Uncle Gabe could. He had once heard Daddy tell Mommy that Uncle Gabe was the smartest man he'd ever known, even if he did insist on acting like a clown most of the time.

Just before he fell asleep, Jason smiled to himself. If Uncle Gabe was that smart, he could help him prove he wasn't pretending. He knew he would at least *try* to help. One of the things Jason liked best about Uncle Gabe was that, unlike a lot of other grown-ups, he was never too busy to help him.

4

Gabe was more irritated than puzzled as he stared at the container which last night had held enough baked ham to provide not only today's lunch, but a topping for two or three pizzas as well.

When he turned to look at the others gathered around the table for lunch, he scowled suspiciously at their innocent expressions.

"Okay. This has gone far enough. It's no longer funny. I can survive on peanut butter and jelly sandwiches the rest of the week if you can."

"What's wrong, Gabe?"

Jennifer's puzzled frown looked sincere enough, but she had learned that deadpan expression of hers from a real pro; nobody was more gifted in the art of the impassive stare than Jennifer's husband and his best friend, Dan.

Jennifer had been a quick study, all right. An example was the way she had successfully convinced him she had nothing to do with the fluorescent-painted sign that had been placed in the middle of the town square a few weeks earlier. Said sign had, in shimmering neon colors, proclaimed the birthday of one *Gable Scott Denton*; his age, and his phone number. Beneath those multi-colored facts blazed an open invitation for everyone to call, "after eleven tonight, please, to give Good Old Gabe your regards."

After days of relentless digging, he had finally confirmed his suspicions: His wife and Jennifer had painted the sign and erected it well after midnight the eve of his birthday. When confronted, Jennifer had given an incredible performance, first pretending to be horrified, then wounded that Gabe would point a finger at her. Not once did the woman actually lie to him; she simply skirted the issue. Only later, when she could no longer stand being left out, did she somewhat gleefully admit her part in the escapade, confessing with what appeared to be a touch of pride that the entire caper had been her idea.

Small wonder that he wasn't the least convinced by the guileless stare she now leveled on him.

He sighed. "The ham, in case there happens to be one among you who's ignorant of the fact, is gone. At least," he said testily, "it's *almost* gone. There might be just enough left to bait a moustrap. No more."

"You're kidding." The lovely Lyss, his wife of mere weeks whom he loved to the point of derangement, now ambled up beside him looking beautiful, curious, and convincingly dumb. He knew his lady well enough, however, not to be taken in by her charm. Love him though she might, she could be every bit as devious as her sister-in-law if she sniffed the possibility of a good chuckle at her husband's expense.

"How could it possibly be gone?" she asked, peering down into the empty plastic storage container.

Dan was next. Gabe would have been disappointed if his routine had not outclassed the combined efforts of all present. He lifted his Roman gladiator chin and with casual disapproval remarked, "How could anyone lose a ham?" The inflection in his voice made it less a question than an accusation.

Jennifer folded her hands primly on the table in front of her, gave Gabe a look of great wisdom, and said, "Probably a 'coon. Or a wild dog. There are a lot of them around here, you know."

Jason was the only one to remain silent, and Gabe

decided he didn't have the heart to question the boy after his grilling about the missing cookies the night before.

This was as good a time as any, Gabe decided, to let them know their fun and games were not going to continue throughout the week. Not without a price.

He gave them his iciest smile and said, in a tone usually reserved for a couple of rambunctious boys in his church youth group, "All right, people. Enjoy your amusement. Just chuckle your way through the bread and butter sandwiches you're going to have for lunch . . . and dinner."

Lyss groaned, but he ignored her. "Sit," he ordered with an imperious nod at the harvest table.

Obediently, she shuffled across the room to join the others. They waited, all eyes riveted on him.

"Now, then," he continued, shifting easily to the role of maligned but forgiving patron, "let's look at the facts. We have a variety of items missing from the storage pantry—linens and assorted groceries. In addition, two dozen cookies and approximately five pounds of baked ham have disappeared within a twenty-four hour period."

When no one offered to comment, he went on. "Since all present have vowed their innocence of any wrongdoing," he paused, appraising each face looking up at him from the table, "the only conceivable answer is that somewhere on the grounds lurks a very clever, very quiet, and fleet-of-foot thief."

There was a heavy moment of silence in the room before Jennifer broke it. "You think it's one of us playing a joke. Don't you?"

Gabe looked at her with a totally bland expression. "Why in the world," he drawled, "would you say a thing like that?"

They continued to argue good-naturedly among themselves for a few more minutes, accomplishing nothing. Finally, with individual sighs of resignation, they put together a generous supply of bologna and cheese sandwiches for their lunch.

They ate quickly and quietly. Jennifer and Lyss exchanged occasional wry glances. Dan, however, Gabe noticed with some satisfaction, appeared to be giving the whole situation serious thought. He was uncommonly silent. So much so that Gabe began to wonder if he might have misjudged him. Certainly he didn't look like a man who was secretly enjoying a practical joke.

No one lost any time returning to their respective jobs at the campers' cabins once they had eaten. Only Jason remained behind, offering to help clean up.

"Well, cub, what do you think about our mystery?" Gabe asked, giving the boy's shoulder a squeeze as they put away the last of the dishes.

Jason studied the blond man's lively green eyes for a moment, then offered uncertainly, "Do you think I made up the children in the woods, too?"

Gabe's smile faded as he sensed that the small, tow-headed boy standing before him was deeply troubled. He wasn't sure how to respond, but Jason was obviously expecting something from him.

"*Did* you make them up?" he countered bluntly.

"No, sir. I *saw* them." He tucked his lower lip beneath his two front teeth.

Gabe studied him. "A boy and a girl, you say?"

Jason nodded.

"And you think they're responsible for our missing food?"

Again, the boy nodded, this time more hopefully.

Gabe began to stroke his mustache with his index finger. The kid was convinced. While he didn't pretend to know much about little boys, he thought he *did* know Jason. And Jason didn't lie. One thing was certain: Jason believed he had seen a boy and a girl coming out of the woods. Deep down, Gabe knew it was probably foolish to even consider the possibility. Still, he had a hunch that it was important to Jason that *someone* believe him. What would be the harm in at least pretending to go along with the kid?

He narrowed one eye and said, "All right, cub. I think you and I might just try to catch ourselves a couple of poachers."

He dried his hands on the dish towel, then slung an arm around the boy, now bright-eyed with excitement. With a grin and a quick hug, Gabe propelled him into the great room.

"What we need," he announced gravely as they sat down beside each other on the slightly sagging couch, "is a plan."

They put their plan into effect shortly after midnight that night.

"I'm cold, Uncle Gabe," Jason complained, pushing closer to him.

Gabe tucked the boy's muffler more tightly around his neck. They were lying on their stomachs just below a rise at the foot of the field, not far from the huge old sycamore tree by the gate.

The night was even colder than the earlier part of the week had been, damp and heavy with the threat of rain or snow. There was no wind, but the stillness seemed to hold more threat than serenity, much like the proverbial calm before the storm, Gabe thought uneasily.

Sneaking out of the cabin unnoticed had not been as difficult as he had feared it might be. Waiting until Lyss was deeply asleep, he had slipped quietly from bed, dressed hurriedly in the bathroom, then crept up the stairs to the loft. Instead of having to wake Jason, as he had expected, he found the boy waiting for him, wide-awake and impatient.

Now, huddled closely together in the brush, Gabe asked him again, "You're sure this is where you saw them? This is where you talked to the little girl?"

Jason nodded, his brown eyes half-hidden beneath the blond, shaggy bangs spilling out from his cap. "I tried to talk to the boy, too, but when he saw me, he grabbed the girl's hand and ran away with her."

Gabe studied his face carefully. "What were they wearing, cub?"

Jason frowned and pressed his lips together. "The little girl had on a bright red coat," he said after a moment. "With a furry hood. The boy's coat was black, with shiny white pockets."

If Jason *was* creating all this from his imagination, Gabe thought, he certainly wasn't sparing any of the details. In spite of his earlier doubts, he was beginning to get caught up in his nephew's story.

"You said the boy looked to be about your age?"

Jason nodded eagerly. "But he's—" he searched for the word he wanted—"*thin.* He's thin, Uncle Gabe. And he has dark hair, almost black, not light like—"

Gabe stopped him in mid-sentence, touching a warning finger to his lips and motioning to the far corner of the field.

Only yards away from where they were lying, a shadow moved from behind the end cabin in the boy's section.

Jason stirred, and Gabe quickly shook his head and put a restraining hand on his shoulder. As they watched, the shadow changed and broadened, then suddenly grew still.

It was difficult to make out anything other than dark, shadowy forms. Only one security light was on at this end of the field, and it was at the girls' side of the cabins. Gabe raised his head another inch or so above the rise, and Jason cautiously imitated him. When there was no sign of movement, Gabe began to wonder if they had seen nothing more than a harmless clump of shrubbery being ruffled by the wind.

Then something moved. Again. His eyes widened with disbelief as not one, but two small figures slowly emerged from the shadows. Jason caught a sharp breath beside him, and Gabe warned him with a quick hug to stay quiet.

Even in the darkness, he knew what he was seeing. *Kids. Two kids. So Jason hadn't made them up after all.*

He held his breath, watching them. They hovered close to the cabins for a moment, as if to make sure no one else was around. Suddenly, they took off, one pulling the other by the hand, in a frenzied run across the field. They were headed in the direction of the main cabin.

"That's *them*, Uncle Gabe!" Jason's whisper was harsh and excited.

Gabe gripped the boy's arm. "Shh! Stay down. Give them another minute, then we'll—"

"*Look!*"

At Jason's muffled cry, Gabe swiveled around to look back at the cabins. Another shadow was emerging, this one much larger. Unbelievably, the figure of a man, crouching low but moving with agile grace, broke out of the shadows between the two cabins at the end and bolted across the field after the children. As he ran, he snapped his head back and forth, as if to make sure he wasn't being watched.

They were too far away to get a good look at his face, but Gabe could tell two things by the way he moved: He was a seasoned runner, and he was no kid.

A needle of fear pierced the back of his neck. Finding out that Jason's "friends" really existed had been a surprise, but not a frightening one. However, the realization that someone was with them—an adult—was unsettling, even alarming.

Who were these kids, anyway? And the guy—he was pretty sure the runner was male—who was he? What possible reason could they have for hiding at an isolated youth camp in weather like this?

"We're going after them," he whispered. "But don't let them see you." He pulled himself to his knees, helping Jason to his feet as he stood. "Until I find out what they're up to, we're going to keep our distance. Understand, cub?"

Jason nodded but tugged on Gabe's hand. "Hurry, Uncle Gabe," he whispered insistently. "We have to catch them!"

Gabe wondered uneasily why he had ever come up with this crazy idea and just what, exactly, he intended to do when they actually confronted the two kids and their unknown cohort. He conceded to himself that this entire scheme might not turn out to be one of his better ideas. Here he was, out in the woods with a nine-year-old retarded boy, chasing after three strangers who could be up to just about anything. The only other adult male he could count on was most likely sound asleep—not to mention the fact that he was also blind.

For one of the few times in his life, he faced a situation in which he could not find so much as a trace of humor. The only thing he could think about was the fact that the three most important people in his life were sleeping innocently, and helplessly, inside the main cabin while some creep and his two sidekicks were prowling around outside. And, as if that weren't enough, the eager little kid at his side, who had also carved out an extremely important place for himself in his heart, seemed to have no idea they might be in danger.

Staying low and out of sight, they reached the main cabin only a moment behind the others. There was a fruit cellar banked against a small rise a few feet away from the cabin, and Gabe ran around to the side of it, motioning for Jason to follow him.

A nearby security light cast enough of a glow on the end of the cabin that Gabe, peering cautiously around the corner of the cellar, could see the furtive trio now standing on the deck, just outside the kitchen door.

He glued himself against the side of the building to avoid being seen, watching with growing anger as the man on the deck, after a quick glance around, took something from his pocket. He inserted it into the space between the door and its frame.

At that point, Gabe realized that he was watching a burglar open the kitchen door with a plastic credit card. To his astonishment, the man stayed on the deck while the two kids went inside.

Furious, Gabe studied the man who now skulked across the deck, surveying one end of the cabin, then the other.

He could see him clearly enough to tell he was young, in his twenties maybe, and appeared wiry and trim in a dark racing jacket and jeans. He was bareheaded, and his hair looked thick and curly.

An impatient tug on his hand reminded Gabe that Jason couldn't see around him. He frowned at the boy, then shook his head to warn him to stay still. Glancing from Jason to the cabin, his mind reeled when he saw the man ease himself carefully through the door.

"Come on," Gabe whispered to Jason. "We're going around to the window."

"What are we going to do, Uncle Gabe?" Jason whispered back.

Gabe shook his head almost violently. He tried to ignore the growing knot of dread in his throat, reminding himself that, if these three were indeed their thieves, the worst they had done so far was to steal some food and supplies. That would seem to indicate that they posed no real threat.

Besides, even if they did decide to make trouble, he thought he could handle two kids and a man who looked to be a few inches shorter and several pounds lighter than himself.

They climbed the steps and tiptoed across the wood deck as quietly as possible. He again moved Jason safely behind him before edging closer to the window.

He found it almost impossible to move without making a racket. His feet felt like frozen clubs in the sturdy hiking boots, and his legs were stiff and unsteady from the cold and nervousness. Carefully, he plastered himself against the wall of the cabin and looked through the side of the window.

At first, he could see nothing. There was no light inside the room, and the faint glow shed by the outside security light was only enough to cast shadows.

Then one of the shadows moved, arcing a thin stream of light from corner to corner across the room.

Gabe stiffened. The man inside the kitchen obviously had a flashlight. *To see what they're stealing?* he thought acidly.

He pressed the side of his face even closer to the glass. The subtle ribbon of light revealed one of the children—the boy—moving toward the storage pantry.

Inching even closer to the window, Gabe tried to get a look at the far end of the kitchen. He stifled a small murmur of disappointment when he saw that the man was standing right beside the door. *So much for sneaking in unnoticed.*

His eyes quickly scanned the room, and he moved in closer so he could see better. There was the little girl, bathed in a soft wash of light from the open refrigerator door. Apparently, she was about to help herself to the contents.

Gabe pressed his lips together in a tight, angry line. At his side, he felt Jason squirm restlessly. He glanced down at him, again warning him with a finger over his lips to remain quiet.

A soft thud from inside made him turn back to the window. He saw that the refrigerator door was shut and the flashlight had been doused.

All movement inside the room had ceased. With a pounding heart, Gabe'e eyes locked on the dark form now standing in the doorway between the kitchen and the great room. Even in the darkness, he immediately recognized the towering silhouette.

Dan! What did he think he was doing, walking right into the midst of those three, when he couldn't even see what was going on . . .

Gabe stared with frightened eyes through the glass, dismayed at the thought that Dan might not even know anyone was *in* the kitchen. Had he heard something and come to check—or had he simply walked into the room and stumbled onto them unknowingly?

Either way, his being there eliminated any chance for delay. Gabe would have liked a little more time to think, but he knew he no longer had that option.

He looked desperately around the deck, hoping to find some kind of weapon. There was nothing but a few empty clay pots and a discarded milk can.

He glanced worriedly at Jason. The boy was huddled against him, shivering. Once more he looked in the window, then across the deck into the dense fort of trees surrounding the cabin.

What do I do, Lord? I need to do something, *but I'm afraid of doing the wrong thing and getting someone hurt . . . that guy in there might even have a gun . . . and there stands Dan, who can't see what's happening . . . and the girls are probably still asleep . . . whatever I do, it can't be wrong . . . .*

His decision made, he told Jason what he wanted him to do, then began moving toward the kitchen door.

5

Daniel immediately identified the sound he heard upon entering the kitchen: Someone had just closed the refrigerator door.

So Gabe wasn't sleeping either. Good. He was wide awake and hungry; might as well have company with his snack.

"Gabe?"

He waited, surprised by the silence.

"Lyss?"

Not a chance. Lyss wouldn't waste her sack time on anything, even food.

Then it dawned on him. "Okay, Jason. Don't try to sneak past me." He walked on into the room. "You'd just better hope there's plenty of that pudding left, sport." He stretched out a hand, waiting for Jason to take it.

Only after a long moment of absolute silence without contact did he begin to sense something wrong. Jason would have come to him, would have at least said something. No, it wasn't Jason in the room with him. Nor was it Gabe or Lyss. The two of them were great pranksters, but they never took advantage of his blindness.

Still another few seconds passed before a warning buzz finally went off in his mind.

There was someone in the kitchen, all right . . . but who?

He seldom used Sunny on harness in the cabin; it was too comfortably familiar. He now wished, however, that he had brought her into the kitchen with him.

His heart skidded to a stop once, then raced. He stood unmoving, hoping he didn't look as frightened as he suddenly felt. The thought reminded him that he didn't even know if the lights were on.

He lifted his chin and forced his voice into a calm authority he didn't feel. "Who's there?"

He waited, his chest tightening. "I said, who's there?"

Silence was his only reply. Yet he was absolutely certain he wasn't alone.

For the first time in months, he was gripped by the same kind of vertigo attack, a dizzying assault bordering on panic, that had so often seized him during those first few months after the automobile accident had blinded him.

The oppressive sensation of being watched, watched by an unknown . . . adversary hit him, hard, leaving him feeling exposed and vulnerable.

If only he could find something to grab onto.

Perspiration bathed his face, and again he reached out, stepping sideways as he did. With relief, he felt the edge of the large, vintage cabinet, clung to it, and waited.

Teddy stood frozen in place only inches from the door. He squinted into the shadows, trying to get a good look at the dark giant now standing in the middle of the room.

Silhouetted in the glow from the outside light, the guy looked huge, with shoulders broad enough to block Teddy's view, and arms that, even in a bathrobe, spelled power.

He glanced at Stacey, hoping she wouldn't panic. In the dim glow filtering through the room, he could see that the poor little kid looked like someone had thrown an electric current through her system. Her dark eyes were round and frightened, her mouth half-open with terrified astonishment.

Nicky, ducking his head out of the storage pantry at the sound of a strange voice, reached his little sister's side in three wide steps and hunched himself protectively between her and the big guy in the bathrobe.

For the second time, the giant spoke. "I said, who's there?"

Obviously, he couldn't see too well in the dark. Teddy fleetingly wondered why he hadn't turned on the lights, grateful that he hadn't. One thing was certain—they had only seconds in which to move if they were going to get out.

With one hand, he threw the door open, then jumped aside, yelling, "*Run! Now!*"

The words were no more than out of his mouth when a blond guy in a blue ski jacket hurtled through the open door, blocking the kids' flight with his body.

Stacey, unable to avoid crashing into the man at the door, hit him hard enough to make her bounce and reel backward. She started to cry.

With a strangled exclamation of fury, Nicky charged the man and began pounding at him with his fists. But the man easily grabbed both of the boy's wrists with one hand and pushed him firmly against the wall.

Flipping the light switch with his other hand, he called out, "Dan—are you all right?"

Teddy took a step toward the door, and the guy in the ski jacket barked at him, "*Freeze*, buddy! Don't even blink!"

Teddy looked at him. He didn't see a weapon, but something in that level, green-eyed stare stopped him.

"Gabe?" The big man in the white bathrobe looked relieved. Relieved and bewildered. "What's going on? Who's in here?"

Without taking his eyes off Teddy, the one called Gabe snapped, "Fagin and friends. But instead of picking pockets, they're looting the kitchen."

The dark-haired man looked even more puzzled. "What are you talking about?" His frown deepened as he turned in

Stacey's direction. "Who's crying?"

Teddy studied the bearded man in the robe with dawning understanding. *The guy was blind!*

He felt like crying. They could have sneaked out! If it hadn't been for that macho blond character, they could have got away without anyone being the wiser. He made a choked sound of disgust, and the guy in the ski jacket eyeballed him with a mean look.

Suddenly the room exploded with noise as a large golden retriever came charging into their midst, snarling and barking like a wild thing.

Teddy's stomach kicked over when he saw the dog home in on him, roaring her intention to attack. Instinctively, he lifted his arm across his throat.

Stacey, still crying hard, screamed in terror.

The blind man stopped the dog with a sharp command. The retriever dug in with all four paws, lowered her head, and silently continued to challenge Teddy with a menacing stare.

"Stacey," Teddy was dismayed at the weak sound of his own voice. "It's okay, baby. Be quiet, now."

She looked at him, her dark eyes uncertain, her tear-tracked face pinched and frightened. Gradually, she quieted to a less frenzied sobbing, but she continued to watch Teddy with an anxious gaze.

Just then a good-looking woman in a furry emerald robe came racing through the door, running up to the blind man and grabbing his arm. "Daniel! What's wrong? I heard—"

She turned her eyes from him to scan the room, her mouth falling open in confused amazement as her gaze came to rest on Teddy, then the children.

Teddy's head swiveled when another woman came marching out of the room behind the kitchen. She was tall, with hair the same unusual charcoal color as the blind man's. She was wearing a plaid bathrobe a couple of sizes too big for her, and she looked irritable and sleepy.

"Gabe, what is going on out here? Do you guys have any idea what time it—"

She stopped just past the doorway, staring blankly at the assembly in the kitchen, shaking her head as if to clear it.

Dazed and frightened, Teddy's mind began to whirl at the outrageous confusion in the room. He felt as if he were in the middle of an old Marx Brothers' movie, doing one of those off-the-wall scenes where everybody's talking at once over a barking dog and crying kids. He half-expected someone to walk up and hit him alongside the head.

The sassy-looking lady in the fuzzy green robe broke into the bedlam with a sharp voice. "Where's Jason?"

Jason? Teddy looked at her. *How many people were crammed into this place anyway?*

The blond guy answered. "Outside. In the fruit cellar. I told him to stay there until I came after him."

"The *fruit cellar?*" she repeated, her brown eyes widening with disbelief. "Why in the world did you put Jason in the fruit cellar?"

"Later, Jennifer," he snapped. "Right now, let's find out what's going on with our . . . *guests* here. I'll fill you in on the details later. Don't worry. Jason's fine."

"Well, for goodness' sake, I'm not going to leave him out there in the cellar!" she said, her eyes flashing with anger. She started to move toward the door, but the blind man reached for her.

"Don't go out there alone, Jennifer—"

She shrugged out of his grasp and went on, stopping at the door to rake Teddy's face with a look of incredulous fury. "There can't be anything *outside* to worry about, Daniel. All the trouble seems to be in *here!*" She slammed the door hard on her way out.

It was quiet for a long moment, as if most of the excitement in the room had followed her outside. The only sound was Stacey's choked weeping.

Gabe looked at the girl, then turned to Nicky. "Is she your sister?" he asked sharply.

The boy leveled a hostile stare on him and nodded, saying nothing.

"Then take care of her," he ordered curtly.

With interest, Teddy noticed that Gabe's eyes, hard with anger only a few minutes before, softened as he watched Nicky go to his sobbing little sister and try to comfort her.

Nicky put his arm around Stacey, then coaxed her to sit down on the long bench behind the table. Pulling a handkerchief from his pocket, he pushed it at her, saying, "Stop crying now, Stacey. And blow your nose."

As if surprised to hear his voice, she quietened. She looked up at Nicky, then down at the crumpled handkerchief in his hand. After a second, she twisted up her mouth and said, very distinctly and with obvious distaste, "It's not clean. I don't want it."

Nicky scowled. "It's the only one I have. Use it."

Hearing the gruffness in his voice, she puckered her bow-like mouth and began to cry all over again.

Gabe looked at her for a moment, then, keeping one eye on Teddy, moved to the large white cabinet beside Dan and opened the bottom door, tearing off a paper towel from its rack.

He walked over to Stacey, stooped down, and offered her the towel. "Here. This is clean."

The little girl raised her eyes to the slender, blond-haired man before her. She studied him thoroughly for a few seconds, then reached out a small, mittened hand and took the towel, dabbing awkwardly at her nose. With her other hand, she pulled the hood of her coat down, away from her face, revealing two stubby pigtails protruding from either side of her head as if they'd been glued into place.

Still wiping her nose and staring at Gabe, she asked in a soft voice, "Please, may I have Mrs. Whispers?"

He frowned. "Who?"

She pointed across the room, where a slightly battered-looking rag doll lay on the floor in front of the refrigerator.

Awareness dawned in Gabe's expression, and he went over and picked up the doll. When he returned and handed it to her, Stacey immediately hugged the doll fiercely to her heart. "Thank you," she said with surprising dignity between sniffles.

As if he couldn't help himself, Gabe allowed a faint twinkle to spark his eyes. "Why did you name her Mrs. Whispers?" he asked.

She studied him. "It's a secret," she said gravely. "I can't tell you."

A smile tugged at the corners of his mouth, and he nodded. "Right."

Teddy saw his expression sober as he walked over and started talking in a hushed tone with the blind man, probably, Teddy thought, to brief him on the situation in the kitchen.

A stab of anger sliced through Teddy as he looked at the kids. Anger at himself for being stupid enough to get caught like this. These people would call the police, of course. And that meant further delay in getting to Virginia. His jaw tightened as he realized how little protection the local police would be. There wasn't a community police force in the country that was any match for the Family's soldiers.

His gaze went to the door when it opened. The woman in the green robe walked in, holding the hand of a small boy in a heavy coat and a knitted cap. The thatch of blond hair Teddy could see escaping from the child's cap was almost white, but the boy had eyes as dark as his own. He seemed to be about Nicky's age, but when he spoke, his speech sounded like that of a younger child. Of course, Nicky talked more like an adult than a nine-year-old, so Teddy couldn't be sure.

"That's them, Mommy! I told you! Didn't I tell you?"

He pulled free of the woman and marched up to the other two children. "Why did you run away from me? And why did you break into the cabin? Were you stealing from us?"

Nicky's eyes darkened with hostility. "We weren't *stealing!* We were just borrowing what we needed for a couple of days. We were going to pay you back."

"Jason—" The blind man reached out a hand. "Come here, son."

The boy went to him, but he continued to look back over his shoulder at Nicky.

The blind man put his hand on the boy's shoulder. "Jason, are these the children you saw? The ones you tried to tell us about?"

"Yes, sir," the boy replied excitedly. He looked at Teddy. "I didn't see *him*, though. Just the children."

Teddy studied the blind man. The woman had called him "Daniel." The name somehow fit the man, Teddy thought. Strong. Solid. Teddy sensed that, blind or not, the big man standing in the middle of the room was very much like his name.

Daniel suddenly turned in Teddy's direction, as if he knew exactly what he was thinking. "Who are you?" he asked bluntly. "What are you doing here?"

Teddy was uncomfortably aware that everyone in the room—including the children—was staring at him. Even the blind man seemed to be looking right through him with his piercing blue eyes.

"I think you owe us an answer," Daniel said quietly. "And I think you'd better make it quick."

Teddy pulled in a long, resigned breath. "My name is Teddy Giordano."

"And the children?" the blind man prompted. "Are they yours?"

When Teddy hesitated, Gabe moved a little closer to him and said, in a voice thick with antagonism, "They're not, are they? What are you doing with these kids?" His eyes raked Teddy's face suspiciously.

"They're not mine," Teddy admitted. "But I didn't take them against their will, if that's what you're thinking."

"You don't even want to know what I'm thinking," Gabe countered, his face hard and cold.

The two men stared at each other for a long moment, then Teddy looked away. His gaze went to Nicky and Stacey, who were looking at him with frightened but still trusting expressions.

"We're in trouble," he said shortly. "Bad trouble."

"You sure are, buddy." Gabe's voice was deadly calm, but Teddy could almost feel the heat of the man's anger as he turned and started toward the other room. "I'm going to call the sheriff, Dan."

"*No!*" Teddy instinctively jumped toward him, and Gabe whirled, his eyes glinting with an unmistakable challenge.

Teddy continued to move closer to Gabe, looking from him to Daniel. "Wait. Please don't call the police. It'll only make things worse for us."

"I just bet it will, friend," Gabe said sarcastically.

"Look, I know we shouldn't be here. But it's not the way it looks—"

"Right," Gabe sneered. "You were just making a late-night delivery."

"Why don't you just *listen* to him, Mister?" The boy, Nicky, turned on Gabe. His black eyes burned with frustrated anger behind silver-framed glasses. "We're not thieves."

"My mistake, kid," Gabe said harshly. "Where I come from, people who steal are usually called thieves."

The boy's angular jaw tightened, and with one finger he pushed his glasses up a notch on the bridge of his nose. "We're just trying to stay alive, Mister!"

Ignoring him, Gabe turned back to Teddy. "What are you doing with these kids, anyway?" he asked. "Where are their parents?"

Without warning, the little girl jumped up from the bench and ran across the room to Teddy. He bent down and scooped her up in his arms.

"It's all right, baby," he murmured against one pigtail. "It's going to be fine. Don't cry anymore, okay?"

"Gabe asked you a question," the blind man said quietly. He hadn't moved, and the dog, settled by his master's side, continued to stare at Teddy guardedly. "Where are the parents of these children?"

Again, it was Nicky who hurled an answer at him.

"They're *dead!* All right? What else do you want to know?"

A small muscle just below the faint scar at Daniel's left eye twitched as he turned his face in the direction of Nicky's voice. "Both of your parents are dead, son?"

"Yes," the boy hissed at him. "Both of them."

Teddy could feel the barely controlled fury emanating from Nicky.

"Nicky," he cautioned, "stay cool."

Then he turned to Gabe. "Look—I've got money. I'll pay you for what we've used. I admit we took some food. And blankets and pillows." He dug his wallet out of the back pocket of his jeans. "Here, take this," he said, peeling off a roll of bills without even counting them and shoving them at

Gabe, who shook his head in refusal.

"You'll pay, all right, buddy. But not *your* way," Gabe said acidly.

Teddy glared at him in frustration.

"Are you in trouble with the police?" Daniel asked abruptly.

Teddy turned to him and uttered a small, harsh laugh. "I *wish*."

Daniel frowned. "Then who?"

After a long pause, Teddy said, "You don't want to know, Mister. Believe me, it's better that you don't know."

"You said you're in trouble," Daniel stated calmly. "Bad trouble." He paused. "Isn't that what you told us?"

Teddy hesitated, then nodded, forgetting the man couldn't see. "Yeah," he mumbled. "That's what I told you."

"Then you need help," Daniel said simply. "You and the children."

Teddy looked at him. It suddenly hit him that the big man's face reminded him of Nick. There was the same unexpected blend of kindness and strength, gentleness and humor, that had marked Nick Angelini. Missing from this man's features, however, was the gruffness, the tough, weary mask that years of frustration, anxiety . . . and crime . . . had baked into Nick. Nick had once told Teddy his whole life had been like a big spider web—a web he had woven and in which he had trapped himself with his own youthful foolishness and greed.

It was crazy. They were strangers . . . but Teddy suddenly knew he could trust this man.

Before he could answer, Daniel spoke again. "We can't help you unless you tell us the truth."

Gabe and the two women were staring at Teddy. Hard stares, expectant and suspicious. Teddy knew he had to answer them—and that what he was about to do was unfair to the seemingly good people in this room. He felt one sharp sting of guilt at the jeopardy in which he was about to place them, aware that ignorance was the only real defense against the Family.

But his guilt took second place to desperation. He *had* to get the kids to safety. And if there was the slightest chance that these people could help them, he had to take it. Nick's kids were at stake. He had promised Nick. He had to do everything in his power to keep that promise.

Turning back to Daniel, he said flatly, "You're right. Let's talk."

6

It was after three in the morning before they finally called it a night.

Long before then, Jennifer and Lyss had found sleeping bags in the storage pantry, then settled all three children in the loft bedroom.

Now the adults sat in the silence of the great room, drained from hours of talking and occasional arguing. Once in a while, someone would take a sip of lukewarm coffee or glance uneasily at the person next to them. Mostly, they looked at Teddy Giordano, studying him, appraising him, wondering about him.

Not for the first time since Teddy had begun to tell his story, Daniel shook his head in a bemused gesture. "You've been here for nearly four days."

Teddy nodded, then again remembered Daniel's blindness. "Almost. We spent most of Saturday night in a motel just outside Morgantown. When I spotted the limo on our tail Sunday morning, I just picked a road and started flying until I shook them. We found this place late that afternoon. I saw the sign on the main highway," he explained, "and took a chance on finding somewhere safe to hide. I knew I wouldn't lose them for long if I stayed on the road."

"Where's your car?" Daniel asked.

"I hid it in the woods. Covered it up with some tree branches and stuff. It's Nick's car, not mine—a big silver limo, hard to miss. But I think I've got it out of sight."

Fatigue seemed to enfold him as he rubbed his hands down both sides of his face and uttered a weary sigh.

Jennifer watched him, wondering how old Teddy Giordano was. Probably not as old as he looked, she thought. With several days' growth of beard and his dark eyes hollowed by shadows, he appeared unkempt, haggard, and exhausted. Looking at him, thinking about the incredible story he had recited to them, she found it hard to stay angry with the man.

Still resting his head in his hands, he said, "I never intended to stay this long." His words shot out in a fast, staccato barrage that strengthened Jennifer's original impression of a tense, anxious person beneath the somewhat arrogant facade.

Dropping his hands to his knees, he continued. "I thought we'd hole up for a day or so, just until I was sure it was safe to leave again. But before you got here Sunday night, I tried to call the number in Virginia—the number Nick gave me. I found out that the man I need to talk with is in Florida until the end of the week." He lifted his hands, palms up, and shrugged. "I didn't know what to do. I decided our best bet was to just dig in here and wait."

"Are you aware that the little girl is running a low-grade temperature?" Lyss asked him shortly. "Has she been ill?"

Teddy frowned. "No. At least, she hasn't said anything. I found one of those small electric heaters in the pantry," he admitted. "I thought it would take care of that little cabin."

Lyss softened her tone somewhat and said, "You're certainly resourceful. She may just be tired. Some kids do that, run a fever, when they're tired or upset. But she ought to stay warm and get some rest."

Frustration lined Teddy's face even more deeply. He flushed, then turned back to Daniel. "Look, I *am* sorry . . . about everything. My intention was to leave plenty of money behind us to pay for whatever we used. I'm no thief."

Jennifer heard an edge in Daniel's voice when he

answered, even though his tone was pleasant enough. "You've been in the end cabin all this time? What if one of us had just walked in on you? We've been working our way down the entire row of cabins since Monday, cleaning and getting them ready for spring campers."

"I always knew where you were," Teddy said without hesitation. "I had your routine down. I figured you weren't going to get to us much before Friday. Besides, all we had to do was go out the back door and we'd be in the woods. That's one reason I picked the cabin on the end." He paused. "When the kids told me about your little boy seeing them the other morning, though, I held my breath the rest of the day, wondering if you'd come looking for us."

"Unfortunately," Daniel replied, a look of regret crossing his face, "no one believed his story. At least, not at first." He lifted his chin, frowning as if something had just occurred to him. "Two nights ago, late, Jennifer and I both heard a child crying. Was that—"

"Stacey," Teddy finished for him. "We, ah, we were leaving the fruit cellar, and she forgot her doll. She went back to get it, and when she ran to catch up with us, she fell." He glanced down at the floor. "She got scared, started crying . . . she was pretty upset."

Jennifer saw Teddy flinch when Gabe snapped, his tone knife-sharp with disgust, "No *wonder* the poor kid is sick! You've had her running around after midnight every night in thirty degree temperatures! What do you expect?"

Slowly, Teddy raised his eyes to Gabe, answering his outburst in a harsh, defensive tone. "We had to eat. And there was always someone around in the daytime. What was I supposed to do?"

Instead of answering, Gabe merely glared at him, uttering a soft sound of contempt.

"I think we can understand why you did what you did,"

Daniel interjected calmly, as if he sensed a brewing confrontation between the two men. "And I don't see much point in belaboring the right or wrong of it; it's done. But I've got to tell you that I think it would be a mistake to take those children out of here right now."

Jennifer bit her bottom lip, anticipating an explosion when Gabe half-rose from his chair. His usually fun-filled eyes glinted with surprise and angry disbelief.

Without giving him time to interrupt, Daniel went on to explain. "You don't know exactly when this federal marshal will be back. You don't even know but what these . . . people who were following you aren't still around somewhere." He frowned as he leaned forward on his chair. "Do you really think you ought to take any more chances with those children?"

Teddy raked a hand through his dark, badly tousled hair. "What else can I do?" he countered. "The kids are tired; they're scared. I need to get them settled somewhere. And I *have* to get to that marshal. Once I deliver the notebook, Sabas will lose interest in the kids and me. They're only after us now because I have something they want."

Daniel shook his head. "I wouldn't be too sure of that. They probably think you can make some fairly accurate guesses about who killed your boss, too. They may even think the children know something." Saying nothing more, he let the significance of his words hang between them.

Teddy stared at him, his face pinched and pale. His voice wavered when he replied. "All the more reason I have to get the kids to a safe place soon."

Jennifer watched him clench his hands together and crack his knuckles, once, then again.

He looked at her. "Their mother died of cancer four years ago," he said tightly. "Now they've lost their father, too.

They're hurting. They're afraid. I've got to get them settled somewhere. They need a home. They're just kids . . ."

It was then that Jennifer decided she liked Teddy Giordano. True, she had seen some negative character traits in him over the past three hours. He came across as being somewhat self-indulgent. He was sporting a watch that must have cost hundreds of dollars and a diamond ring that flashed its four-digit price tag every time he lifted his hand. His boots were obviously Italian, his jeans designer, and his sweater imported cashmere.

She had already detected more than a hint of arrogance in his manner, and she suspected a touch of the con man as well, a clever one, most likely. In addition, he seemed defensive, high-strung, and cynical. Despite all the minuses, however, she couldn't quite see him as an evil man. Instead, she felt a sense of intelligence, a bold but generous spirit, and a great deal of loyalty.

When he looked at those children—even when he talked about them—his defiant dark eyes softened to an expression that looked very much like love. Jennifer decided that anyone trying to harm the Angelini children would have to get Teddy Giordano out of the way first.

Daniel's voice broke into her thoughts. "Why don't you get yourself a sleeping bag out of the storage pantry," he suggested to Teddy, "and sack out with the kids upstairs for a few hours? Tomorrow morning is Thursday. You can try your man in Virginia again first thing." He paused. "Frankly, I think what you need to do is wait right here until someone comes for you and the children. You might be placing all of your lives in danger by leaving here."

"And he'll undoubtedly be placing *ours* in danger if he stays." Gabe got up, crossed the room, and stopped directly in front of Teddy, staring at him with open resentment. His eyes never left Teddy's face, but his words were directed at Daniel.

"Are you really buying all this, Dan? The guy's admitted being part of the *mob!* He could have *kidnapped* those kids, for all we know." His usually smiling face was taut with outrage. "Who knows what we'll bring down on our heads if we let them stay here?"

Daniel gently released Jennifer's hand and stood up. He walked slowly over to the fireplace, where a low flame was still flickering, and stood, his back to the fire. "You think we should make them leave? What about that little girl and her brother?"

Jennifer watched Gabe carefully. The tension between him and Teddy had been obvious from the beginning. She doubted if either of the two men recognized the reason for the current of resentment arcing between them. Most likely, she thought with a touch of irony, it was a case of one con man bumping heads with another.

Gabe, of course, had long ago put his cynical, somewhat abrasive nature to rest, burying it when he made a decision to live for Christ instead of for himself. But that didn't mean he couldn't recognize the coat—and unconsciously react—when he saw it hanging from another's shoulders.

When there was no reply to his question, Daniel quietly prompted, "Gabe?"

He looked at Lyss once, then Jennifer. With a weak little grimace of defeat he said, "Obviously, we can't just kick the kids out in the cold. And if they stay, I suppose *he* stays."

When Jennifer looked at Daniel, she immediately knew he was fighting a smile. He and Gabe had the most totally *open* friendship she'd ever witnessed. They could read each other with an almost uncanny accuracy. And Daniel was reading Gabe at this very moment. If Jennifer didn't miss her guess, he knew that his friend was softening—at least a little—but felt compelled to make the protests in keeping with his image.

"If you think I'm wrong, Gabe, say so. You and Lyss have as much at stake here as we do."

Unexpectedly, Teddy broke the exchange by hauling himself up off his chair, saying, "I'll settle it for you. He's right. If we stay, we jeopardize all of you." He flicked an almost apologetic look at Gabe. "There's no reason you should stick your necks out for us. We'll go," he stated wearily. "As soon as the kids get a couple more hours of sleep, I'll—"

Gabe didn't let him finish. He faced Teddy, his eyes narrowed in challenge. "Don't be stupid. Your choices aren't all that great, Giordano. You owe those kids whatever protection you can give them." His gaze swept Teddy's face with disdain. "Dan's right, unfortunately. You'll have to stay."

The two men stared at each other without blinking until Teddy finally inclined his head in a reluctant gesture of agreement. "All right." His eyes were distant, his tone grudging when he mumbled, "Thanks."

Jennifer understood where Gabe was coming from, even though she doubted that Teddy could. Dear Gabe—so much in love with Lyss, his new wife, so wholly dedicated and loyal to his best friend and brother-in-law, Daniel—he would give up his life for anyone in this room, including Teddy Giordano.

But as unselfish and caring as he was, he could also be hard and unyielding when the people he loved were threatened. She sensed that Teddy couldn't possibly understand Gabe's kind of love, a combination of toughness and tenderness, gentleness and strength.

When Gabe asked his next question, Jennifer half-expected Teddy to tell him it was none of his business.

"Exactly how involved were you with these goons anyway?" His expression was suspicious. "This guy you worked for—was he some kind of . . . godfather or what?"

Teddy looked as if he were about to smile, then seemed to think better of it. "It's not quite like the movies. No, Nick had a lot of power, but he was no *padrone*. He was what you've probably heard called a *capo*—a boss, a chief."

"And I suppose you were one of the Indians?" Gabe asked caustically.

Teddy shrugged. "I was his driver. Kind of a right arm to him, I guess. I drove the limo for him, raced a couple of his cars, worked on them, that kind of stuff. And I helped out with the kids—took them to school, to the doctor, the dentist, all that." With a level look, he added, "If you're asking was I into the action . . . no. Never. Nick made a point of never letting me near the business."

"How long had you worked for him before . . . his death?" Daniel asked.

Teddy thought for a moment. "Nine, ten years, I guess. Since I was about sixteen. I worked part-time in a garage he owned when I was still in school. When I graduated, he took me off the street, gave me a job with him at his house."

Daniel nodded thoughtfully. "So you were close."

Teddy glanced away, and Jennifer saw a look of great pain cross his face before he hardened his expression. "Nick Angelini was good to me," he said flatly, his tone making it clear that he would say no more.

The room was silent for a long time. Finally, Daniel moved away from the fireplace and walked to Jennifer, holding his hand out to her. "I think we're all in agreement about what has to be done. But before we turn in, let's pray about this."

Jennifer took his hand and rose from the couch. She saw Teddy dart a startled and embarrassed look at them.

After a moment's hesitation, Gabe took Jennifer's other hand, then Lyss's. It was Daniel who offered his hand to the stranger in their midst, waiting until Teddy, with obvious reluctance, joined them in their circle.

Although Jennifer kept her eyes closed the entire time Daniel prayed for their "new friends," she was sure she could feel Teddy Giordano's troubled gaze studying each of them.

She found herself wondering if the young man with the haunted, anxious eyes had ever heard anyone pray before. She clasped Daniel's hand more tightly, grateful as always for the strength and the goodness of the man standing next to her, and for the blessing of the family into which she had married.

She smiled to herself when Daniel gently squeezed her hand as if he knew exactly what she were thinking . . . and praying.

7

The snow began shortly after dawn the next morning, falling from a sky that looked like a piece of lead-colored canvas. Moderate at first, by midmorning it had increased to the kind of treacherous, wind-driven snow familiar to natives of the mountains. Heavy and threatening, it came down fast. As it fell, the air grew more and more bitter with angry gusts of wind and flying frost.

The children cheered, but the grown-ups looked at each other with worried eyes. While Jennifer paced the floor, Lyss set the table, only half-listening to Gabe, who seemed to talk a little faster each time he looked out the window. Eventually, Daniel began to drum his fingers on everything he touched, a sure signal to his wife that he was, if not tense, at least preoccupied.

During breakfast, Jennifer coaxed Gabe and Lyss into helping her clean the last two cabins on the boys' row. Teddy and Daniel agreed to stay with the children who were begging to go out and play in the snow.

By eleven o'clock, Teddy had tried his call to Virginia three times.

Daniel heard him sigh with frustration when he returned to the great room after his last attempt.

"Still no answer?"

"No. I must have let it ring twenty times." He paused. "I don't know what to do."

Daniel was on his knees in front of the fireplace, trying to fix the stretcher on an immense old rocking chair beside the hearth. It had been his grandfather's favorite chair, then his father's, until Lucas had finally surrendered to his wife's plea to "retire" it. When he did, Daniel had immediately claimed it for his own.

"Not much else to do but wait," he said now, half-turning toward Teddy's voice. "Give me a hand here, will you? Just hold this steady for a minute."

Teddy braced the chair, watching Daniel force the stretcher back into its opening.

Daniel stood up, wiping his hands on his jeans and smiling at the sounds of laughter coming from outside. "Sunny's still in the yard with the kids, isn't she?"

Teddy glanced out the window. "She sure is," he said, smiling when he saw the retriever spill Stacey onto the snow and then push at her with her nose until the little girl giggled out loud. "I think they're playing hide-and-seek. And I'd say your dog is winning."

"You don't beat Sunny at hide-and-seek," Daniel replied with a grin. "That's her favorite game." He walked over to the large pine table beside the couch and picked up his coffee cup, grimacing when he found it empty. "Lyss said Stacey's temperature was normal this morning."

"Yeah, she's fine," Teddy said warmly. "Are you two related, by any chance? You kind of look alike."

"Lyss and I?" Daniel smiled. "She's my kid sister."

"I thought so," Teddy said with a small nod. "Is she a nurse or something?"

Daniel shook his head. "No, she's a phys ed teacher." He started toward the kitchen. "Let's get some coffee. I think Gabe made a fresh pot before they left."

Teddy followed him to the door to the kitchen. He watched as Daniel made his way to the stove, noticing that he seemed to be counting off his steps. When he saw him lift the coffee pot, he moved to help, then stopped. Obviously, the blind man knew what he was doing.

"There should be some clean mugs on the right hand side of the cabinet," Daniel said, filling his own cup, then setting the old-fashioned porcelain coffee pot back on the stove before walking across the room to sit down at the table.

Teddy got his coffee, then went over and slid onto the bench behind the table. He glanced outside to check on the kids, then stirred cream into his coffee, studying Daniel as he did. For a fleeting instant, he sensed something familiar about the man across from him. The feeling passed, but his curiosity sharpened.

Daniel Kaine had an unusual face, he thought. An interesting face, but not an easy one to read. He supposed women would find him good-looking, but Teddy thought he was more . . . compelling. He had a presence that caught your attention, made you wonder about him. His dark, bronzed skin was that of a man who spent a lot of time outdoors. His deep blue eyes were strangely unnerving, seeming to follow the slightest sound or movement in a room.

It was a strong face, Teddy thought again, just as he had the night before. Even beneath his heavy black beard, Daniel's jaw looked firm, his chin slightly stubborn. His dark brows were generous but not severe, and his nose was prominent, stopping just short of being hawk-like. Teddy noted the small, vertical scar at his left eyebrow and the almost startling streak of silver running randomly along the left side of his thick charcoal-colored hair.

When Daniel lifted his arms above his head and stretched, Teddy had a sudden, peculiar sense of a tightly harnessed power, a dynamic but fully controlled energy. It was at that moment the memory hit him.

"*Daniel Kaine!*"

Surprised, his arms still stretching upward, Daniel lifted his dark brows in a question.

"I *knew* there was something familiar about you!" Teddy said excitedly. "I saw you on TV when you won the gold medals in the Olympics. You're the 'Swimming Machine'—isn't that what they called you?"

Daniel lowered his arms, a half-smile crossing his face. "You remember that? You couldn't have been very old when I was at the Olympics."

"Oh, man! Do I remember? You were *great!*" Teddy exclaimed. "I was in junior high, but I'll never forget it." His words tumbled out with boyish enthusiasm. " 'Course, you didn't have your beard then, and you weren't . . . " He broke off, embarrassed.

Daniel, however, only smiled. "No, I grew the beard later. It's easier than shaving in the dark."

"Can you . . . I mean, do you still swim?" Teddy asked without thinking, then realized he might be out of line.

But Daniel didn't seem to mind. "You bet I do. Every day. I've got an indoor pool in my home," he explained easily. "That's why I'm feeling kind of stiff right now, going most of the week without any exercise."

"How long—" Teddy stopped, floundering, again wondering if he should ask the question on his lips.

"How long have I been blind?" Daniel finished for him mildly. "About six years now."

Teddy stared at him, feeling a strong wave of sympathy wash over him. This man had been a national figure just a few years ago, an athletic hero. Now he was blind. He was blind and doing odd jobs in a youth camp. Talk about lousy luck.

"So, you work here now, huh?"

Daniel started to take a sip of coffee, stopped, then smiled. "Well . . . just this week, actually. The couple who manage the Farm haven't had a vacation in a long time, so we came up to give them a break. As a matter of fact, we've been trying to find another full-time assistant for Mac—he's the manager of the camp—but until we hire someone, we're going to be helping out as much as we can."

"What is this place anyway?"

Daniel then explained the idea behind Helping Hand and filled Teddy in on how the Farm operated.

"Then this is your place? I mean, you own it?"

"Not really," Daniel corrected him. "It's been in my family for years, but now it's owned by several people. When my Uncle Jake decided to retire, a group of people from my church agreed to help finance a camp if Gabe and I would get it going."

"So it's strictly for handicapped kids?"

Daniel nodded. "Some of them stay here several weeks out of the summer, others just come for a week or two. It's worked out so well that we've almost outgrown our facilities. We're trying to buy more land so we can expand, and, as I told you, we're going to add to the staff."

Teddy shook his head with appreciation. "It's a great idea. But none of you live here?"

"No, we live in Shepherd Valley—that's about sixty miles from here. I run a Christian radio station there."

"A *Christian* radio station? What's that?"

"It's a radio station with a Christian programming format," Daniel explained. "The music we play—our talk shows—all of our programming is Christ-centered."

"I see," Teddy mumbled. He didn't, but he didn't have any desire to be enlightened either. That prayer circle last night had been enough for him. These people were obviously church people, and church people always made Teddy uncomfortable. Not that he would take Daniel to be some kind of a fanatic. He seemed to be okay. But he must be into religion pretty heavy if his *job* was even Christian.

"Is there money in that?" he asked abruptly.

Daniel laughed. "Not much, I'm afraid. But we make a living. I do some counseling part-time, too. We get by."

They both smiled when they heard Stacey squeal with excitement, followed by the boys' laughter.

"I was really fortunate, having the station to go back to after the accident," Daniel said, continuing their conversation. "At least I didn't have to train for a new job. A lot of blind people have to take on a whole new career, and believe me, that's rough." He paused, then went on. "Learning to live without your sight is enough of a challenge. If you have to learn a new job, too, you've just got double trouble."

Teddy was quiet for a long time, thinking. His voice was soft when he finally spoke. "Yeah, I'm sure that's true. But I'll tell you, Daniel, there are times when the idea of a whole new beginning sounds pretty good to me."

"Oh?" Daniel looked interested.

Teddy glanced out the window without answering. He could see Stacey down on her knees with her arms around Sunny's neck, giggling as the retriever nuzzled her chin. Jason and Nicky seemed to be hitting it off great, he noticed. Heads together, the two boys seemed to be deeply absorbed in a pile of rocks before them. *Nicky's probably explaining what they're made of,* he thought wryly.

He turned back to Daniel. "Sometimes I wish . . . " He stopped, surprised at what he was feeling. "Sometimes I wish I could just . . . be a different person. Start all over, from scratch. A brand new life." He laughed at his own foolishness. "Crazy, I know."

Smiling, Daniel shook his head as if he understood. "Not so crazy. There are a lot of people in this world who feel the need to start over. It's not such a bad idea, you know. Sometimes it's the only thing to do."

Teddy uttered a small, humorless laugh. "And sometimes," he said bitterly, "it's the only thing you *can't* do. Your past is your past, man. And it's always with you."

"Unless you're willing to give it up," Daniel replied.

Teddy looked at him, but said nothing. They were silent for a long time, both locked in their own thoughts. Teddy found himself thinking about his past, especially about his family.

Things hadn't been so bad before his dad died, he remembered. He and his older sister, Gina, had always had to work to help out at home, but their parents had been decent to them. His dad had died, however, when Teddy was only eleven, and a year later his mother remarried. Jack Falio had immediately judged his new stepson to be a "wise-mouthed kid," a "son with no respect."

At the same time, Gina had married and left home. Feeling deserted by his sister and betrayed by his mother, Teddy made no effort to understand or accept his new stepfather's domineering, old-country ways. Within weeks, the two of them were trapped in a split relationship that would never mend. When his new little half-sister came along, Teddy started drifting further and further away from his mother and the home that, by then, had come to seem like a prison.

For the next two or three years, he spent most of his time on the street with a relatively harmless gang. Later he picked up pocket money by doing odd jobs at a garage owned by Nick Angelini. "Nicky Angel," the other *capos* called him.

Nick didn't spend much time around the garage, but he kept a close eye on his employees, even a part-time flunkie like Teddy. For some reason, the older man took a liking to the defiant teenager, eventually putting him to work full-time, even letting him race a couple of his cars professionally. Finally, he asked Teddy to move into his home and become a kind of "personal assistant" to him.

Teddy didn't have to be asked twice. In spite of the fact that

Nick was a known boss for P.J. Sabas, Teddy was in awe of the big, good-natured Sicilian. If Nick had tried to put him into the business, he wouldn't have hesitated. He looked up to Nick, trusted him, and tried his best to please him.

Surprisingly, though, Nick made it clear from the beginning that Teddy was to stay clean. He took him under his protection, much as he would have a son or a younger brother. The closest Teddy ever got the action was if he happened to overhear an occasional phone conversation between Nick and one of the other *capos*.

He knew what Nick's business was, and he knew it was dirty business. But he told himself it didn't matter. In his own way, Nick was a good guy. He was good to his kids, good to Teddy, good to his friends. So he was mixed up with the mob. So what?

Daniel's voice startled him out of his thoughts. "So what would you do, Teddy, if you could start over again? What kind of life would you choose for yourself?"

Teddy looked at him. He was surprised at how easily he could answer Daniel's question. It was as if he had thought it all out, which he never had. Not really. It was just that sometimes, over the years, he would daydream about the way he'd like to live. If he could.

"I'd get out of the city, for starters," he said. "I grew up on the streets, and I hated it. The noise, the smell, the traffic. One reason I liked it at Nick's so much was that we lived outside town. It wasn't like this, you understand, on a farm and all; but at least the air was cleaner, and it was quiet most of the time." He hesitated, then added almost shyly, "I even had a garden."

"A garden?"

"Yeah. A *good* one, too. The kids helped me. We had flowers on one end and vegetables on the other. It was a beauty."

"So you like being outside. What else? If you could start over again, I mean?"

Teddy smiled to himself. "It's pretty wild, I guess."

"Some of my daydreams are, too." Daniel leaned back, crossing his arms comfortably over his chest, waiting.

"Well . . . I know it's impossible—" Teddy stopped, then went on, "—but if there were any way I could, I'd . . . adopt the kids. Nicky and Stacey." He waited, expecting Daniel to laugh. Or maybe even frown in disapproval.

Daniel did neither. Instead, he dropped his arms and leaned forward, resting his hands on the table in front of him. "That doesn't really surprise me, Teddy. I hear your love for those children in your voice every time you talk to them. Or about them."

Teddy swallowed hard. "Yeah . . . well, we both know it's never going to happen. But you're right. I really do care about the kids. They're like my own, you know? And I think they care about *me*, too."

"Yes," Daniel answered softly. "I believe they do." After a moment, he said, "You know, Teddy—there *is* a way you can start over again. Oh, you might not have everything you want just the way you want it, the way you've dreamed about having it. But if you really decide you want a fresh beginning, there is a way to do it."

Suddenly, Teddy knew what was coming. He tried to stop it. "I suppose you're talking about being a Christian."

Daniel looked surprised. He leaned back in his chair, a small frown creasing his forehead. Finally, he nodded and said, "Yes. That *is* what I'm talking about."

"I've already heard that stuff, Daniel," Teddy countered quickly. "I know the whole story, man. By heart."

Now Daniel looked genuinely puzzled. "You do?"

"Yeah. Nora—that's Nick's housekeeper—she was all the time preaching at me. And the kids. She took them to church every Sunday, and she did her best to get me there, too."

"But you didn't cooperate?" Daniel asked with a faint smile.

"No, I didn't. I went to church when I was a kid. And to Bible school. I know the story, about the cross and Jesus and all that."

"But you don't believe it?" Daniel was still smiling, and Teddy couldn't quite figure out why.

"Believe it?" Teddy hesitated only an instant. "No. No, I don't believe it."

"What part of it don't you believe, Teddy?"

Teddy dragged in a deep breath. He didn't want to make this man angry. He *liked* him. And, without knowing why, he wanted Daniel Kaine to like *him*, too. "Look, Daniel, where I come from, men don't *die* for each other. They *kill* each other."

His words fell heavily upon the silence between them with the dull thud of reality.

Finally, Daniel nodded. "I see your point."

Teddy hadn't expected that. "It's just not for me, that's all," he muttered.

"That's where you're wrong, Teddy," Daniel said quietly. "It *was* for you."

"What?"

Daniel released a small sigh. "I think I know where you're coming from. If you felt that your life was everything it should be, you wouldn't feel the slightest need to change it. Right?"

Teddy nodded, caught himself, then mumbled a sound of agreement.

"But because you think your life *isn't* what it should be, you don't believe you have any part in Jesus, or that He has anything to do with you?"

Again, Teddy grunted his assent.

"You just can't quite swallow the story that one man would climb up on a cross and die for another man, especially an . . . unworthy man."

Teddy looked at him.

"Keep in mind, Teddy, that Jesus wasn't just another man. He was God . . . God in the flesh. When He did what He did, He was showing us a different kind of love . . . His kind of love. And the kind we're supposed to have for one another."

Something about the assurance of the man got to Teddy, making him almost angry. "Nobody—*nobody*—willingly puts their life on the line for someone else! If you believe that, man, you've been out of the real world too long! Maybe, just maybe . . . if Jesus *was* God, like you say, He would do it. But *if* He did it, it wasn't . . . for people like me."

"Very rarely will anyone die for a righteous man, though for a good man someone might possibly dare to die."

Not yet realizing that Daniel was quoting Scripture, Teddy said, "That's what I'm saying . . . "

"But God demonstrates his own love for us in this: While we were still sinners, Christ died for us." Daniel finished softly.

Teddy blinked, saying nothing.

"That's His Word, Teddy . . . not mine."

Teddy started to interrupt, but Daniel stopped him. "Wait. Bear with me. This is for you, Teddy. '. . . *It is not the healthy who need a doctor, but the sick. I have not come to call the righteous, but sinners to repentance.'* Wait," Daniel held up a restraining hand as if he could see Teddy's attempt to protest, "there's more. *'He died for all . . . ' All*, Teddy. No exceptions. One more, okay? *'Therefore, if anyone is in Christ, he is a new creation; the old has gone, the new has come!'*

"Now isn't that exactly what you're talking about?" Still, he didn't give Teddy the opportunity to answer, but went on in the same casual, good-natured tone. "It surely sounds to me," he said meaningfully, "as if God wrote the answer before you ever asked the question."

Abruptly, Daniel stood up. "I'm going to loan you Jennifer's Bible—mine's in Braille," he said with a smile. "Maybe you might like to pass a little time today by reading through the Gospel of John." He started to leave the table, then turned back. "If you're a fast reader and want to find out more about this subject of new beginnings, go on to Romans."

"The Bible's hard for me to understand," Teddy said grudgingly.

Daniel grinned at him. "You ought to try reading it in Braille sometime, friend," he said dryly. Counting off his steps, he walked out of the room.

8

By early evening, the tension in the cabin was almost tangible, especially between Gabe and Teddy.

Jennifer knew Daniel was also feeling the strain. Earlier he had confided to her that he was particularly bothered by the fact that the snow had begun just after dawn. He had told her that both his grandfather and his Uncle Jake were men who knew these West Virginia mountains as well as they knew the inside of their own homes, and they always insisted that the worst snowstorms were those that began shortly after the first light of day. Daniel had admitted that their observations weren't infallible, but immediately added that he had seen enough mountain winters in his own time to be wary of the storm now in progress.

Under ordinary circumstances, being snowed in with her husband and family wouldn't have bothered Jennifer in the least. To the contrary, it would have been fun. Present circumstances, however, were anything but ordinary.

Even the normally imperturbable Lyss had a flinty edge in her voice, Jennifer thought uneasily. Only the children seemed reasonably untroubled by their situation, although she had caught Nicky staring apprehensively out the window a couple of times.

Hour by hour, the day had trudged by into evening, clouded by a peculiar overtone of unreality. They did their work, ate their meals, made the obligatory small talk, and all the while avoided too frequent mention of the snow that continued to fall in a steady curtain of white.

At seven forty-five, Teddy again tried to reach someone with the Federal Witness Program. Jennifer was surprised but relieved when she heard him begin a conversation. When he returned to the others at the far end of the great room, however, she thought his cheerfulness seemed half-hearted.

"At least I got an answer this time," he said with an uncertain smile.

"That's good," Daniel said. "What did you find out?"

"I still didn't talk with Nick's contact," Teddy replied. "But the man who answered *is* a federal marshal, and he seemed to think the marshal who arranged everything with Nick is back in town. He promised to have someone call me within the hour. He said if he can't connect with the other marshal, he'll make the arrangements himself to get us out of here."

"That should make you feel better," Jennifer said, trying to smile. She and the children were sitting at a small table in the corner, stalled in what seemed to be an endless game of Monopoly. Stacey was too young to comprehend the strategy, yet insisted on being a part of the game, and Jennifer was too restless to concentrate more than a few minutes at a time. Consequently, Nicky had captured the board long before.

And now the children were getting tired. Tired and irritable. Jennifer could hear it in their voices. *And Gabe isn't much better,* she thought. He was as feisty as she'd ever seen him. She sighed, then brightened a little when Daniel suddenly pushed himself up out of his rocking chair, saying, "Let's make some music. It's too early to go to bed, and it's too quiet in here to stay awake."

Ignoring the silence that greeted his suggestion, he pushed up his sweater sleeves and said firmly, "Come on now. We're not going to stop the snow by sitting around worrying about it. Lyss, have you finished that dulcimer for Jennifer yet?"

"Mm."

"If that was a yes, go get it. Gabe, where's your fiddle? Jason, will you find my guitar for me, please? And get your Aunt Lyss's banjo, too."

Jason suddenly came to life, hopping off his chair and running to the corner of the room where Daniel's guitar and Lyss's banjo were propped against the wall.

With the help of the three now wide-awake children, the adults also seemed to find a reserve supply of energy. While Gabe tuned his fiddle, Jennifer oohed and ahhed over the new dulcimer her sister-in-law presented to her.

Gabe even managed a civil comment to Teddy when the younger man, admiring the finely crafted, hourglass shaped instrument in Jennifer's hands, looked at Lyss with awe and asked incredulously, "You *made* that? I thought stuff like that was only made in factories." He stopped. "What *is* it, anyway? Some kind of a guitar?"

"Same family, but older," Gabe told him. With evident pride, he added, "Lyss custom-makes them for people."

Teddy looked from the dulcimer in Jennifer's lap to Lyss with open admiration. "What's it sound like?"

"Show him, Jennifer. Jennifer plays a lot better than I do," Lyss explained. "I just like to make them."

Jennifer began to pluck the four-stringed, sweet-voiced instrument softly. "The dulcimer is thousands of years old," she said, continuing to play as she spoke. "It goes all the way back to ancient Persia. The immigrants who settled here in the mountains brought it with them from Europe."

"The thing about Lyss's dulcimers," Gabe said, "is that no two are alike. She gives every instrument she makes its own unique personality—its individual voice."

"Just like the Lord makes people." Daniel turned toward Teddy as he tuned his guitar. "He made each one of us exactly the way He intended us to be." He stopped, his smile softening when he added, "You know, it never fails to amaze me how God can take a few discarded scraps of a life and shape it into something brand new and beautiful."

Jennifer, by now accustomed to Daniel's unexpected analogies, glanced from her husband to Teddy, then back to Daniel. She sensed a definite current between the two men, nothing hostile, but some kind of . . . *challenge,* perhaps.

Continuing to pluck the dulcimer lightly, she smiled warmly at her sister-in-law. "Lyss, it's beautiful. It's *exactly* what I wanted!"

"Sing, too, Mommy," Jason begged, plopping down on the hearth and motioning for Nicky and Stacey to join him. Teddy followed the children over to the fireplace, dropping down beside Stacey and settling her snugly against his side.

Jennifer began to play and sing "Wildwood Flower," a sad old folk ballad about lost love. After a moment, Daniel added his guitar and started to hum, then sing along with her.

They sang another mountain love song before Lyss and Gabe joined in with their instruments. The four of them then harmonized on church camp choruses, encouraging the children to sing with them. Eventually, they played a little bluegrass, then turned to hymns before ending with a number of folk songs.

When they finally stopped, Stacey tugged at Teddy's sweater sleeve. "Teddy, could I have a fiddle? Like that one?" She pointed to the fiddle in Gabe's hand.

Jennifer smiled at the sleepy-eyed little girl. Her stubby black pigtails were sticking straight out from either side of her head, and her round face was flushed with heat from the fireplace.

"Maybe when you're older, baby," Teddy said, giving her a hug.

Stacey's face fell, but brightened when Gabe made a beckoning motion with his hand. "Come here, kiddo. You can play my fiddle."

Jennifer looked at him, wide-eyed, then glanced at Daniel, whose dark brows had also shot up with surprise. Gabe's fiddle was no ordinary instrument. It had been handcrafted by a master in North Carolina for an absolutely ridiculous amount of money, and it was Gabe's pride and joy. No one other than Daniel or Lyss dared to touch it, and even they were scrutinized by its owner's eagle eye the entire time it was out of his possession.

Now he was inviting a six-year-old *child*—a child he barely knew—to play it?

Stacey squealed and went sailing over to Gabe, beaming with delight as he allowed her to rake the bow awkwardly over the strings of the fiddle. Jennifer was fairly certain that high-pitched screech sliced Gabe's spinal cord in half, but she gave him credit for being a good sport.

She saw Daniel shake his head and grin. Lyss, too, was gaping at her husband as though she didn't believe what she was seeing.

"No, no—you don't *push* the bow, dumpling—"

Dumpling? Daniel choked, then coughed, and Jennifer could have howled at the look of amazement on his face.

"—You draw it gently over the strings. Like that. That's it, good! That's great. Try it again. Gently, remember. *Good!* You're doing fine!"

Jennifer rolled her eyes at Lyss, who continued to stare at her husband with astonishment.

"—Wait, wait, careful, now. You don't want a *harsh* tone, dumpling. You want a nice, even, *sweet* tone. Like this."

The feeling of contentment in the room, the warmth from the fire, the children's laughter, Daniel's occasional dry comments and Lyss's good-humored replies, all worked together to lull Jennifer into a comfortable, drowsy tranquility.

Suddenly, the mood was shattered. A loud, jarring bark from Sunny and the combined cries of the children made everyone jump with alarm as the room plunged into darkness.

Still clutching her new dulcimer, Jennifer sprang up from the couch, startled by the unexpected darkness and noise.

"What is it? What's wrong?" Daniel put down his guitar and got to his feet.

Reaching for him, Jennifer exclaimed, "The lights went out, Daniel!"

He found her hand and gave it a reassuring squeeze. "Probably too much weight on the power lines."

The faint light from the fireplace enabled them to see just enough to move around, but it threw the room into eerie, menacing shadows.

Sunny stirred restlessly beside Daniel, and Stacey began to whimper.

His voice gentle, Gabe attempted to soothe her. "It's okay, dumpling. It's the snow, that's all. Don't be afraid." Pulling her onto his lap, he began to rock her slowly back and forth.

Jennifer heard a thump, then a muffled exclamation as Jason pushed up between her and Daniel.

"I hit my knee!" he mumbled, taking hold of Jennifer's hand. "Are you okay, Mommy?"

She smiled at the protective note in his voice and bent to plant a kiss on top of his silky thatch of blond hair. "I'm just fine, honey. I'll take a look at your knee when we get some light in here. Don't be scared."

"I'm not scared," he replied. Then, in a much softer voice, he added, "This is kind of what it's like to be blind, isn't it, Daddy?"

Surprised by the boy's quick insight, Jennifer watched as Daniel smiled and clasped Jason's shoulder.

"Yes, it is, son. Although I imagine you can see a little bit with the light from the fire."

"I wouldn't like being blind, Daddy," Jason said gravely.

"Well, Jason, I don't like it very much either," Daniel admitted. "But I've learned to get around fairly well in the dark. So right now, I want you and Sunny to stay here with your mother for a few minutes. Uncle Gabe and I will get some oil lamps and candles from the storage pantry, okay?" He gave Sunny a command to stay and faced in Gabe's direction.

Gabe, however, was unable to pry himself free from the frightened Stacey, so Lyss followed Daniel to the kitchen.

"I suppose there's a lot of snow on the lines," she said as they moved across the room.

"Probably. How deep do you think it is by now?" Forgetting to count his steps as they talked, Daniel stumbled against the side of the cabinet. He muttered a small grunt of surprise, then went on.

"Gabe said he thought we had at least eight inches after dinner, maybe more."

"And that's been a couple of hours. Is it still coming down?" He stopped as they reached the door to the pantry.

"I'll look out the window."

After a moment, she returned to his side. "Heavier than ever," she said in a thin voice.

Hearing her unease, Daniel tried to reassure her. "There should be plenty of candles in the pantry. What about oil lamps? Do you know where they are?"

"There's one in each bedroom, I think. And a couple in the great room."

"There's plenty of wood. Gabe and I brought in several loads yesterday."

"We're going to need it tonight, without any furnace." She paused. "Dan?"

"Hm?"

"I'm a little worried."

Surprised, he draped an arm around her shoulder. "What's the matter, Pip?" It was a pet name he had given her when she was still a little girl, a name he seldom used anymore. He had heard the edge of fear in her voice, however, and for a moment, she was no longer a grown, married woman, but his little sister again.

When she didn't answer him, he said, "Lyss? What is it?"

"I don't know." She suddenly sounded very young. "I have . . . a really bad feeling. Like something awful is going to happen."

Daniel's heart made a tremendous lunge, then slowed. Lyss was probably the most unflappable person he knew. She was a rock. Lyss simply didn't have *nerves.*

"It's been a strange day," he offered weakly. "With our unexpected . . . visitors, and the storm . . . now the power going off . . . "

He jumped when she clutched his arm. "Dan, I'm afraid."

In the silence following her tense admission, a burst of stormy wind rattled the window pane. Daniel had a sudden sensation of being assaulted by a blast of dark water. He was keenly aware of an enormous, dense *weight* pressing down on him, and he shuddered against the feeling of being engulfed by . . . something. For a terrible moment, he felt Lyss's fear become his own, felt her panic turn into a wave of dread inside himself.

He clenched his jaw and shook his head, drawing in a shaky breath of relief when he felt the wall of foreboding finally ebb and disappear.

"You know what you've got, Pip?" He tried to laugh but, instead, winced at the tremor he heard in his voice.

"What?" She continued to grasp his arm.

"You've got Grandma Lou's heebie-jeebies. You know, the creepers."

She forced a small laugh. "You think that's all it is?"

He nodded and squeezed her hand. "That's what it sounds like to me."

"I suppose you're right."

"Hey, big brothers are never wrong. You ought to know that by now," he teased, giving her a hug.

"I guess I'm just tired," she said, her voice now a little stronger. "Let's find some candles. I don't do so well in the dark."

"Relax," he said dryly. "You're with a pro, remember?"

The night's combination of high wind and heavy snow equalled nearly zero visibility. Boone squinted nervously into the darkness as the windshield wipers pushed the snow first to one side, then the other, grinding with the effort.

The scene outside the car had an eerie, surrealistic quality. The limousine's headlights seemed to project a nightmarish rough cut of film onto the darkness, one distorted frame at a time.

"What're we gonna do, Wolf?" Boone's voice trembled badly, as did his hands on the steering wheel. "It's just about impossible to see *anything* out there!"

"Pull off the road," Wolf said grimly. "I want to look at this map a minute."

Searching desperately for a safe place to pull over, Boone

went another quarter of a mile before spying a small house with a driveway that looked halfway plowed. Carefully, he slowed the limo to a crawl and turned into the driveway, letting the engine idle while Wolf studied a highway map.

After a moment, Wolf looked up, glancing out the window on his side, then leaning forward to look past Boone's head, out the driver's side.

"What do you suppose that is?" he muttered, staring at a sign only a few feet ahead of them on his side of the road. *Helping Hand Farm—10 Miles.*

The black and white sign was barely visible because of the blowing snow. Boone peered through the windshield, frowned, then shrugged without answering.

"Let's find out," Wolf said abruptly. "Get back on the road. I'll help you watch for signs."

Boone looked over at him. "Wolf, if it ain't right on the highway, we'd better not even try to stop," he said petulantly. "If we get off the main road tonight, we may never get back on."

Saying nothing, Wolf returned his attention to the map, glancing up again a moment later to lift his eyebrows at Boone in a "What are you waiting for?" look.

Muttering under his breath, Boone started to pull back onto the highway. The wheels spun, and he glanced pointedly at the man beside him. He tried again, and this time the powerful limo moved backward, lurching only once as it bumped onto the road.

"Relax, Boone," Wolf said, without looking at him. "And go slow—I don't want to miss this place. If the snow gets much worse, we may need somewhere to hole up for the night. Whatever this Farm is, let's not announce our arrival. Let's just drop in unexpectedly."

9

While Jennifer and Lyss placed lighted candles and oil lamps around the great room, Daniel stoked the fire, adding more logs and punching it up to a roaring blaze.

"We'd better call the power company before things get any worse," he said to Gabe as he replaced the fire screen. "Maybe they can send someone out by morning if we get our names on the list."

Gabe secured a candle in its holder and set it on the table by the couch. "I'll call," he told Daniel. Crossing to the other end of the great room, he began to leaf through the telephone directory.

Jennifer settled all three children in front of the fireplace. Taking one of the oil lamps, she started toward the kitchen, stopping when she saw the look on Gabe's face.

"What's wrong?"

He held the handset out in front of him, scowling at it. "The phone's dead."

She looked at him, then the telephone, an expression of dismay crossing her face. "Try again."

It was no use. He tapped the plunger a few times, then shook his head glumly as he replaced the handset on the hook. "Nothing," he told her, his face clouded with uneasiness.

Daniel walked over. "I heard," he said grimly. "I was afraid of that."

"Afraid of what?" Lyss asked from across the room.

Gabe hesitated before he answered. "The phone's out."

Jennifer watched Lyss as she walked toward them, surprised to see that she looked worried. She bit her lip, feeling her stomach tighten with concern. If *Lyss* was worried, maybe their situation was more grave than she had first thought.

"What are we going to do?" Lyss touched Gabe's arm, her eyes fixed on his face.

He took her hand and tucked it under his arm. "We're okay, babe." He managed a tight smile. "Relax."

"Gabe's right," Daniel seconded. "We've got the fireplace, plenty of food—and we'll probably have power in a few hours."

"I don't think so, Dan."

Gabe's flat disagreement seemed to surprise Daniel. "Why not?"

"We're going to have well over a foot of snow by morning, if it keeps up," Gabe explained tightly. "No one's going to get through to restore service in this kind of a storm."

"So we wait," Daniel said with a shrug.

Jennifer studied his face, wondering if he really felt as confident as he sounded. Nervously, she realized she was counting on Daniel to remain unruffled. And Lyss. The two of them were always so steady, so cool-headed, that when either showed the slightest sign of being flustered it seemed to affect everyone around them.

She looked at Gabe, but he was staring across the room at Teddy and the kids. When his gaze finally met hers, his expression was troubled and thoughtful.

He glanced at Daniel, pressing his lips firmly together in a look of decisiveness. He drew in a deep breath and said, "Dan, I'm going to take the Cherokee and go into town."

"*What?*" Daniel exclaimed in disbelief. "Are you *crazy?* You said yourself we're working on a foot or more of snow."

"The Cherokee will get me through."

Jennifer saw a momentary expression of alarm cross Daniel's face. "No, Gabe. You can't risk it."

Jennifer didn't like Gabe's announcement any better than Daniel did. "Gabe, he's right. You *can't* go out in this—"

She stopped when he turned to her. She had seen that expression in Gabe's eyes before. A hard, implacable look, a mixture of withdrawal and resolution. He was going.

Abruptly, he turned, flicking his gaze to Teddy and the children, who were still sitting in front of the fireplace.

"Giordano, will you come over here a minute?"

Teddy said something to Stacey, then stood up and walked across the room.

"The phone's out," Gabe told him shortly. "That means you can't get your call."

At Teddy's look of concern, Gabe went on, his voice as hard as his eyes. "I'm going to drive the Cherokee into town and let the phone company and the power company know we're cut off out here. If you want, I'll call that federal marshal again and explain what's going on. Maybe he'll give me an idea when someone's going to come for you and the kids." As an afterthought, he added, "They're going to need some directions on how to find us, too."

Teddy looked at him. "I'll go with you."

"No," Gabe replied quickly. "You stay here. In case Dan needs some help."

Jennifer watched as the two men locked gazes. Teddy backed down from something unreadable in Gabe's stare.

"All right, sure."

"*I'm* going with you." Lyss said it quietly, but Jennifer heard the note of steel in her voice.

Gabe whirled around. His jaw tightly set, he frowned stubbornly. "No, you're *not*."

Lyss was nearly as tall as her husband, and she met his

eyes with a level gaze. "I am going with you, Gabe. You're my husband, not my keeper, so don't use that tone with me." She stopped, then added, "I couldn't count the times I've heard you say that nobody in their right mind would venture out alone in a heavy snowstorm."

"She's right, Gabe," Daniel said quietly. He turned toward Lyss. "But *I'll* be the one to go with him, not you."

Lyss faced her brother, her blue eyes so much like his, and now flashing with irritation. Even at five-ten, Lyss still had to look up to Daniel. She did so now, studying his face for a moment before she told him, in a tone firm and steady with resolve, "Daniel, he's my husband. And I'm going with him."

Daniel opened his mouth to argue, then closed it, inclining his head in a gesture of understanding. "It's for you and Gabe to decide."

"You can be every bit as hard-headed as your brother, do you know that?" Gabe challenged, looking at her with exasperation.

"As you've so often told me, love," she said easily, turning to walk away, "it's a family trait. I'm going to change into warmer clothes. You'd better do the same."

He watched her all the way out of the room before turning back to the others. "Give me that phone number," he said to Teddy with a sigh.

Teddy pulled his wallet out of the back pocket of his jeans and fumbled under his credit card holder until he found a small yellow slip of paper. "Here. If someone answers, repeat this number before saying anything else. The man you'll talk with is named Keith." He paused. "Tell him to try and get someone here as soon as possible."

Gabe's faint smile was unpleasant. "Oh, don't worry. I have every intention of asking for rush service."

Daniel touched him on the shoulder, then reached out his

hand. "Gabe? Are you sure you ought to do this?"

After an instant's hesitation, Gabe took Daniel's hand. "It's just going to get worse, Dan. And the longer I wait, the more difficult it's going to be to get out of here."

Still gripping his hand, Daniel nodded shortly. "You don't think you'll have any trouble making it into town?"

"The Cherokee's a tank, you know that. The old girl will take us anywhere we want to go." He attempted a laugh. "Relax, man, you're makin' me nervous."

Daniel, too, tried to smile as he withdrew his hand. "Okay. But be careful, you hear? And get back here just as soon as you can."

"Right, boss. You guys have a good time babysitting now." He glanced across the room at Stacey, who was half-asleep in front of the fireplace, her head bobbing against her brother's shoulder. A ghost of a smile flickered, then died, as he turned to leave the room.

Watching him go, Jennifer shuddered and clasped Daniel's arm. "Can't you stop them? I don't think they should go, Daniel." She felt ill at the thought of Gabe and Lyss exchanging the safety of the cabin for the storm outside.

He took her hand as Teddy walked away, leaving them alone. "I don't like it any better than you do," he said, his voice rough with emotion. "But I'm afraid Gabe's right. Someone needs to get us some help before it gets any worse. We don't know how much longer this storm's going to last." His tone gentled. "It's probably not a good idea for us to be isolated out here. Not with these children to look after."

Jennifer tightened her grip on his arm. "Daniel . . . you don't think there's any way those people who are looking for Teddy and the children . . . could find out they're here, do you?"

He pulled her to him and smiled teasingly. "Haven't you

got enough to occupy that busy mind of yours?" His expression sobered. "Nobody's going to be out in this if they don't absolutely have to be, Jennifer. I don't think you need to worry about that."

She leaned against him. He was probably right. But when another gust of wind howled against the side of the cabin, she shivered and drew even closer into the security of his arms. She wasn't certain which bothered her more, the worry of being isolated in the middle of a mountain storm—or the fear that they might *not* be as isolated as they thought. Either way, they could be in serious trouble.

10

The night was made even more vicious by remembrance of the cabin's comfortable warmth, its soft glow of cozy security quickly obliterated from sight.

Outside, the world was a nightmare, an angry, bawling gale of shrieking wind and ice-bearing snow that burned their eyes and singed their skin. By the time Gabe and Lyss made their way through the snow to the garage, they felt as if they had been outdoors for hours.

The Cherokee was cold, too. Gabe turned the ignition key once, twice. On the third try it caught. He waited impatiently for the engine to warm up.

They sat in silence, both trying to ignore the wind lashing the frame walls of the garage. Finally, Gabe switched on the heater. Seeing Lyss shiver at the sudden blast of cold air, he turned it on low.

"You're sure you want to do this? It's not too late to change your mind," he offered, glancing over at her.

"I'm going," she said quietly.

"Crazy lady," he murmured, his eyes crinkling with affection. "Come here." He reached out his hand to her.

A smile rose slowly in her eyes as she looked at his hand, then at his face, now gentle with the tenderness of his love for her. She moved into his arms, and he gathered her against him, saying nothing for a long moment, simply holding her.

"I was afraid you were angry with me," she whispered against his cheek.

"No, babe," he said softly, moving to touch her lips with

his in the gentlest of kisses, his hands going to her face. His eyes caressed her, reassuring her and loving her.

"I love you, Lyss," he whispered. "I love you so much it makes me crazy sometimes."

He felt her catch her breath as he held her gaze, blinking hard against the tears in his eyes. That happened to him sometimes when he held her, sometimes just when he looked at her. Even though it seemed that he had loved her forever, there were times when his love became too big, too overwhelming to hold back the force of it. It would spill over from his heart and explode from his soul into tears of almost unbearable happiness.

He kissed her again. Wishing he could somehow put all his love for her into that kiss, he knew no one gesture, physical or emotional, could ever begin to convey the depth of his feeling for her.

Finally he released her, touched her cheek just once with the palm of his gloved hand, then slid back behind the steering wheel. He looked at her with a shaky smile, making a feeble attempt at humor as he cracked, "We'll want to try that again later and see if we can get it right, Alyssa."

She smiled tenderly at him, then said dryly, "Unless you want to take us both out with carbon monoxide, love, you'd better get this vehicle out of the garage." Fastening her seatbelt, she reminded him, "Buckle up."

He backed out of the garage, then slowly and cautiously began to plow the four-wheeler down the narrow lane he had partially cleared, without telling anyone, earlier in the evening.

"So this is where you disappeared to after dinner," Lyss observed, glancing over at him.

"I put the blade on the tractor and took a couple of swipes at it. Thought it might be a good idea to open a road to the gate, anyway."

They reached the foot of the hill, went through the double gate and started up the unpaved road toward the highway.

It was almost impossible to see. Without the security lights that usually illuminated the road, the snowy night was a thick black-and-white curtain, distorted and forbidding.

The four-wheeler, however, plugged confidently through the snow, and Gabe finally felt himself begin to breathe a little easier.

He was secretly glad Lyss had insisted on coming along. Who wanted to be alone on a night like this? Not that he was all that worried about getting into town. He and Dan had taken the Cherokee through some pretty severe weather.

He had never shared Dan's love for winter. He was at home in the mountains, and had a native's respect for the magnificence of his environment. But if he were to be completely truthful, he admitted silently to himself, he found these winter storms frightening.

"It's even worse than I'd expected," Lyss said quietly beside him, breaking the twenty silent minutes that had passed inside the Jeep.

"It's rough, that's for sure," he agreed. "But we're doing okay."

She nodded and tried to smile.

"What a week, huh?" He glanced at her quickly, then turned his gaze back to the road. They were nearing the exit to the highway now, and he was feeling more confident. The State Route might be snow-covered—there would not have been any extensive plowing done yet—but it should at least be passable in a four-wheel drive.

Without taking her eyes from the road, Lyss answered, "It's been different." She paused. "What do you think of our unexpected visitors?"

He made a small sound of disgust. "I wish they would have

found another place to camp out."

"You haven't been very nice, Gable." The only time she called him *Gable* was when she intended at least a mild reprimand.

"What, I'm supposed to cozy up to the *mafia?*"

"Teddy's not really mafia," she protested. "I think he's probably a pretty good guy. And the kids are sweet."

He shrugged. "The little girl is. Her brother's a little too wise-mouthed for my taste."

"I should think the two of you would hit it off just fine," she said drolly. "You were every bit as precocious as Nicky when you were a boy."

"How would you know? You were still in diapers when I was a boy."

"Mm. But I was advanced for my age, like you."

He grinned at her, then shot his attention back to the road when he felt the Cherokee lurch and skid. He righted the wheels and pulled onto the state highway, shaking his head in disappointment when he saw the condition of the road.

"Remember how I used to follow you and Dan around when you were in high school?" she asked, her expression reflective.

"Yeah. You were a real pest."

"I bet you never thought then that you'd end up marrying me."

"Hardly. I considered strangling you a few times, but never marrying you."

She grinned at him. "Was I really that bad?"

"You were a brat." He smiled as he remembered the long-legged, too-thin, rather plain teenager she had been.

For years, he had thought of Dan's sister as a kind of younger sister of his own, probably because he spent as much, if not more, time at the Kaine house than he did at his home. To him, Lyss was simply a kid, a fantastic basketball player, and, at times, an incredible nuisance.

The first time he had seen her as a *person*, rather than an annoying extension of his best friend, had been one sultry night during the summer after he and Dan graduated from college. The three of them—Lyss, Dan and himself—had gone to a circus on the outskirts of town. An hour or so into the performance, he and Dan had gone to get popcorn. When they returned, one of the male trapeze artists was standing on the sidelines, openly flirting with Lyss who was seated in the front row.

Gabe's first reaction had been disgust. She was just a kid, after all, and the guy looked to be at least ten years older than she. He wasn't sure whether he was more put out with the performer or with Lyss. She should know better than to carry on like that with a stranger.

As they approached, Dan muttered something about his little sister growing up, and Gabe had looked at her more closely. Lyss was no more than sixteen at the time, and while she hadn't lost all her coltishness, Gabe saw with surprise that she was no longer a kid—and no longer plain. He stopped walking but continued to watch the repartee between her and the trapeze artist. Lyss was coy and somewhat awkward; the guy was confident and smug.

Gabe had been totally unprepared for the stab of white hot anger that suddenly jolted him into motion. He moved, spilling half his popcorn as he bolted, unaware that Dan was viewing the scene with surprise and growing amusement.

Gabe planted himself between Lyss and the trapeze artist. Making a gruff comment about robbing the cradle, his voice had been laced with an unspoken but unmistakable threat. His action caught Lyss so off guard, she was speechless. Only after the circus performer had bombarded Gabe with a stream of foreign language did Lyss regain her composure enough to tongue-lash Gabe for "treating her like an infant."

The Kaine eyes flashing, she sat haughtily between him and her brother for the rest of the evening, leaving Gabe to argue silently but furiously with himself all the reasons he could think of for his uncharacteristic loss of control. To make matters worse, Dan would occasionally glance at his sister, then at his friend, with a look that stopped just short of being a smirk.

That had been the beginning. Somehow, he had managed to wait two more years—miserable years of watching her date a football hero, a swim team captain, and a computer whiz—before facing the fact that, ridiculous and impossible as the situation might be, he was nevertheless in love with Dan's kid sister.

When she graduated from high school, they began to date. Her parents had made them wait that long because of the difference in their ages. Even though Gabe had been just like another member of the family since grade school, he *was* six years older than their only daughter, and the relationship had come as something of a surprise to the Kaines.

Even more surprising—to Gabe, as well as to the family—the relationship endured, surviving Lyss's four years away at college and a year working in Colorado afterward.

Within six months of her return home, though, she was wearing an engagement ring—but only after giving Gabe to understand that they would not be getting married until they had the down payment for their first home in the bank.

Gabe was to learn that Lyss was never in a hurry—and very independent. He was pretty sure they had had the longest engagement of any couple in the history of the county—almost five years. But now, finally, she was his wife, and he loved her in ways he was sure he could never have loved another woman. Lyss had been so many things to him for so many years . . . a kid sister, a buddy, a sweetheart, a confidante, and now his wife. It seemed that they had always been together, had always been a part of one another's lives. And it was good. It was extremely good.

Impulsively, he reached for her hand and squeezed it. "You know what, babe? I think one of the reasons I love you so much is because you're such a good sport."

"That's heartwarming, darling—to know you married me for my sportsmanship."

"Yeah. You're a great basketball player, too."

"And you're such a romantic." She grinned at him, then sobered. "Gabe . . . you *are* happy, aren't you?"

He looked at her. "What brought that on? Of course, I'm happy."

Her smile was tender. "Good. I want that for you. It's what you deserve."

He quirked one eyebrow. "Because I'm such a great guy, right?"

She glanced over at him, and her tone was surprisingly fervent when she answered, "Yes. You *are,* you know. You're a truly good man, Gabe Denton. You just don't allow too many people to know *how* good."

He frowned dramatically and pressed a finger to his lips. "Shh. You'll blow my cover, Alyssa. You know I don't—"

His words died in his throat as he came out of a particularly sharp curve on the narrow highway.

Coming toward them from the other direction was a sleek, dark car. He squinted against the headlights, trying to get a better look, eyeing the limousine as it went past.

Suddenly they slowed, skidding off the highway and bumping onto the snow-covered berm, jerking to a rough stop just before they would have slid into an enormous drift. "What are you doing?" Lyss's head swiveled from Gabe to the side of the road.

"I'm turning around," he said shortly, cutting the wheel with care. He backed up, slid, rocked the Jeep forward and pulled back onto the highway.

"What's wrong? Why are you going back?"

"How many limousines are you likely to meet on this road?" he ground out tightly. "Even in broad daylight in good weather?"

She looked at him, wide-eyed. "You think it's—"

His face was grim. "You bet I do."

"Gabe, be careful. Don't you think we should go into town for help?"

"In this weather it's going to take us another 30-40 minutes to get there. Who knows how long to get help. Maybe another hour to get back. Anything could happen in the meantime. No. We're going back. Now."

The road was a glare of ice, treacherous and unpredictable. But the Cherokee was having less trouble than the limousine ahead of them. Within only a few minutes, the back end of the Lincoln had become visible, and they saw it fishtail twice, swerving dangerously left of center before darting back into its own lane.

Gabe tightened his jaw and gripped the wheel in a death lock, staying just close enough to the limo to be sure he didn't lose them.

Lyss leaned as far forward as her seatbelt would allow. "I can't tell how many people are in it, can you?"

"At least two," he said hoarsely. "Maybe more. It's hard to tell."

"You don't think they're headed for the Farm, do you?" she looked at him. "They couldn't possibly know that Teddy and the kids are—"

She didn't finish.

Starting into a narrow, wickedly sharp turn, Gabe

drastically slowed his speed. He felt the Cherokee start to slide, then caught his breath with relief when the tires once again firmly gripped the road.

"We'll stay far enough behind them so they won't know they're being followed," he said tensely. "But I want to keep them in view just to be sure where they're—"

His sentence died as they came out of the turn. Directly ahead of them, only feet away, the limousine zigzagged and swerved. An oncoming semi, immense and terrifying, was fishtailing. Heading directly toward the limousine, it jack-knifed across the road. The rear part of the trailer was now left of center and out of control.

Gabe gripped the wheel even tighter as he watched the limousine suddenly swerve, veering first to the other lane, then straightening and pulling back, finally skidding off the road, untouched.

Panic slammed against his chest as he realized they were now in the direct path of the truck.

The semi roared down on them, its headlights beaming through the night like the terrified, crazed eyes of a metal dragon gone berserk. Gabe tried to veer left, but they were still on ice. His attempt moved only a small part of the Cherokee out of the way of the truck.

Now they were close enough for Gabe to see the driver's wild-eyed mask of horror in the glow of the four-by-four's headlights.

Lyss's scream of terror was cut off by the sound of crunching metal as her side of the Cherokee folded under the impact of the right side of the semi.

The wheel spun crazily under Gabe's hands. Then the Cherokee went dark, and his mind went blank.

Behind them, safely off to the side of the road, the three men in the dark limousine sat staring at what had nearly been their fate.

11

"I'll see if we can help," Boone said nervously, reaching for the door handle. "It looks bad."

From beside him, Wolf said, "No. We don't stop. Just keep right on going."

Boone swung around, staring at Wolf with disbelief. "We can't do that! We've got to at least see if we can do anything. Those people may be dyin'!"

"Then we can't help them, can we?" Wolf replied with chilling indifference. "Now get out of here. And make it quick, before another car shows up."

In the back, Arno fidgeted uneasily. He secretly agreed with Boone. They should stop. But he wasn't about to argue with Wolf.

"There might not be another car along for hours, Wolf," Boone protested again. "Not in this storm."

"It's a state highway. There'll be other cars. Now, *move!*"

Boone stared at him for another few seconds, his mouth quivering uncontrollably. Finally, he pulled forward. The car slipped, then leveled off, and they went on.

Both Boone and Arno eyed the accident as they drove by, their faces pale and troubled. The semi and the four-wheeler were meshed together in a silent, terrible embrace.

Once they were past the gruesome scene, tomblike silence enveloped the interior of the limousine for a long time.

Finally Wolf turned, and his eyes caught Boone's furtive glance. He smiled. "Turn off up there, Boone—at that sign," he said impassively, again looking back to the road. "Let's find out what this *Helping Hand Farm* is."

Gabe tried to dig his way past the mountain of pain. It held him prisoner, the weight of it pressing down on his head, his shoulders, suffocating him with an unbearable agony. He wanted to close his eyes, to return to the warm sea of darkness where he had been and forget the pain. But there was something he had to do, someone he had to help....

Lyss! Where was Lyss? Why was it so dark? He squinted, shook his head, tried to push himself up. Something held him. He fumbled at his waist to release the seatbelt, surprised by the weakness in his hands. Awkwardly, he ripped the gloves from his hands and tossed them aside.

Lifting his head, he saw the semi crushed against the right side of the car. Then he remembered. He tore the seatbelt from his body and lunged toward Lyss. The pain that ripped through his head at the sudden movement made him reel backward and fall against the seat. He squeezed his eyes shut once, pulled in a deep breath, then moved again, more carefully this time, reaching for her as he moved.

"Lyss... honey..."

He touched her hand, felt a sticky wetness on his fingers.

Blood... Lyss's blood...

He rolled to one knee, ignoring the pain in his head... pulled at her seatbelt, trying to free her... unwilling to look at her... fixing his eyes on the seatbelt... forcing himself not to look any further....

"Oh, Lyss... babe... I'll get you out of this, honey... just hang with me... you'll be all right... you'll be fine, babe...."

Glass... there was glass all over... the floor, the seat, on her lap, her hands, her arms... so much glass....

She made a terrible sound, a rasping, choking sound as though she were fighting for her breath. The belt was free. He made himself look up, slowly, unwillingly... there was so much glass . . . and so much blood . . .

She wheezed, and again she choked, an awful, strangling noise. He felt dizzy, then sick. "Lyss . . ."

A truck approached, then stopped. In the gleam of the headlights, Gabe saw her face. Terror slipped its knife into his heart, and his mouth opened in a savage, silent scream.

12

As soon as Gabe and Lyss left, Jennifer took the children upstairs for bed. Checking on them about an hour later, she found all three asleep. Jason and Nicky had gallantly given the bed to Stacey and her doll. Sunny lay on the floor beside the bed, watching Jennifer as she tiptoed around the room.

After watching them for a moment more, Jennifer extinguished the small oil lamp on the bedside table and went back downstairs.

Daniel and Teddy were sitting in the kitchen where she had left them. A lamp flickered softly in the middle of the table. In its glow, the men's faces looked tired and tense.

"We should try to get some sleep," Jennifer suggested, knowing she was only making conversation. Teddy looked at her with a half-smile and shrugged, while Daniel nodded distractedly, saying nothing.

Earlier she had closed the kitchen curtains. Now she walked to the window, pulled one cotton panel to the side, and looked out.

The snow and ice had formed a glaze on the window, but she could see and hear that the wind was still high, the snow heavy. With a sigh, she dropped the curtain and went to sit on the bench beside Daniel.

He covered her hand with his. "Why don't you go lie down for awhile?"

"It would be useless, Daniel. I'm too uptight. I can't even *sit* still, much less lie down."

"Quit worrying. They'll be all right."

"It's such an awful night . . . "

"Gabe could drive that Cherokee in his sleep, Jennifer."

"But the roads must be almost impassable . . . "

"Honey—"

"I'm sorry." She paused. "How long do you think they'll be gone?"

He shook his head. "It takes half an hour to get into Elkins in good weather. In this . . . " He left his sentence unfinished, lifting his chin alertly. "Did you hear something?"

Jennifer looked at him. "No."

"I thought I heard a car."

"Do you suppose it's Gabe? Maybe they couldn't get through."

Teddy got up and looked out the window. "I don't see any lights."

"Might have been an airplane," Daniel said. He squeezed Jennifer's hand. "How's the coffee situation, kid? Have we drained the pot yet?"

"No, there's still plenty. I'll get you a refill," she offered, getting up from the bench.

He pushed himself back from the table. "I'd better throw a couple more logs on the fire."

"I'll do it," Teddy said. "I need to walk off the kinks in my legs anyway." He turned away from the window and left the room.

Daniel got up and went to stand by Jennifer at the stove. "I wish you'd go to bed, honey," he said, slipping his arms around her waist.

She turned to face him. "I can't, Daniel. Not until Gabe and Lyss get back."

He nodded, lightly resting his chin on top of her head.

Jennifer wished she could shake the apprehension that had been gnawing at her all night. "Lyss was worried, Daniel. I could tell."

His arms tightened around her. He said nothing; instead, he pressed a gentle kiss into her hair. Jennifer buried her face in the warmth of his sweater for another moment, wondering if the night would ever end.

Both of them jumped, startled, when they heard the sound of stamping feet on the deck. Upstairs, Sunny barked once, then again, as someone began to pound loudly on the door.

"They *are* back," Jennifer said, slipping quickly from his arms.

"Wait—" Daniel reached for her, but she was already gone.

Jennifer began talking as she opened the door. "What happened, couldn't you—"

She stopped, staring blankly at the three men who stood looking at her from the other side of the door.

The man in front was thin and pale, but neatly dressed in an obviously expensive topcoat. Behind him stood a bearded middle-aged man, tall and gangling, his parka hanging loosely on him as if he had once been much heavier. The third was moderately tall and broad-shouldered in a dark leather jacket; he had thinning hair and a dark moustache. Snow clung to all three of them, and they looked extremely cold.

"Excuse us, ma'am. We were wondering if we could use your phone?" It was the youngest man who spoke, the one in the Chesterfield coat. "I'm afraid we're hung up in a snowdrift." He rubbed his gloved hands together and craned his neck to look past Jennifer into the cabin.

Daniel had come to stand beside her. "What's the problem?" he asked, putting his hand on her arm.

"We're really sorry to bother you," the same man said, smiling pleasantly. "We must have taken a wrong turn somewhere. We got about halfway down the road leading in here before we realized we were lost. Then we got stuck in a drift and had to walk the rest of the way." He stopped, extended his hand to Daniel, and said cheerfully, "Jay Wolf here."

Daniel merely nodded, not moving. The other man's amiable expression faded, and he dropped his hand to his side.

Jennifer's throat tightened as she watched his odd pale eyes narrow to a cold stare. "I'm sorry," she started to say, "but our phone—"

Daniel stopped her, pressing his fingers more tightly around her forearm. "Where exactly were you headed?"

"Actually, we're looking for some friends of ours who live in the area. It's just that we don't know this part of the country, and the storm has made it nearly impossible to find their . . . farm."

"If they live around here," Daniel answered shortly, "I'm sure we know them. What are their names?"

Irritation flared in the man's eyes as he studied Daniel's face. "Look, couldn't we just use your phone?"

Daniel hesitated only an instant. "I'm afraid we can't help you." As he spoke, he released Jennifer's arm and reached for the door.

It happened so fast, Jennifer was never sure who made the first move. Teddy came back into the room, and she heard him choke off an exclamation behind her. At the same time, the man in the Chesterfield pulled a handgun from inside his coat. His hard kick against the door sent it slamming against the wall, and he and the other two men came charging into the kitchen.

Stunned, her pulse thundering, Jennifer saw that each of the three men had a gun.

"Jennifer—" Daniel reached for her, but the muscular man in the leather jacket stopped him with his gun.

"Move back, big guy—against the wall."

When Daniel didn't react, he rammed the pistol hard into his stomach. "I said *move back! Now!*"

"Stop it!" Jennifer screamed at him. "He can't see you! He's blind!"

All three men froze, their eyes locked on Daniel. But only for an instant. Almost immediately, their attention went to Teddy, who now stood in the middle of the room, his face a taut mask of hatred and fear.

"Well, well . . . " The man in the Chesterfield coat took a step toward Teddy, then stopped, his gun leveled at him. "Will you look who's become a country boy."

Jennifer shuddered at the wide, toothy smile. He looked vicious, almost animal-like.

"You've been bad, Teddy-boy. Very bad." Still smiling, he closed the distance between them.

Teddy stood rigid and unmoving. Jennifer saw his hands clench into tight fists at his sides as he met the other man's gaze defiantly.

For a moment, they stood staring at each other in silence. It was Teddy who spoke first. "What do you want, Wolf?"

The other man's smirk deepened. Unexpectedly, he began to laugh, a high, almost shrill hacking laugh that sounded strangely obscene to Jennifer. Her heart pounding furiously, she stared at him with astonishment.

His expression sobered abruptly, his pale eyes watering as he fixed a contemptuous glare on Teddy. "What do we *want?*" He pressed a finger to the side of his nose and sniffed. "You know what we want, Teddy-boy. We want Nick's notebook." He sniffed again, then added, "And we'd also like to have a little talk with his kids."

"I don't know anything about any notebook, Wolf. Or the kids."

Wolf's eyes never left Teddy's face. "None of that, Teddy-boy. Don't lie to me. I hate it when people lie to me. I'm going to have the notebook. And I'm going to talk with the kids. That's what we're here for." Without warning, his gaze went to Jennifer. "While you're thinking about that, why don't you introduce us to your new friends?"

Teddy looked at Jennifer, his eyes pleading for forgiveness. Then he turned back to Wolf. "This is between us, Wolf. Leave them out of it. They don't have any part in this."

Wolf let his watery gaze play slowly over Jennifer, then Daniel.

Finally, he studied Teddy, then smiled again. "You're in a lot of trouble, Teddy-boy. Kidnapping is heavy stuff."

Teddy gave him a startled look. "What are you talking about?"

Wolf shrugged, playfully tipping his gun to Teddy's chin. "Nabbing two kids that don't belong to you—" he shook his head with mocking regret, "—that's kidnapping, Teddy. The feds are looking for you, boy. You'd better let us help you."

Teddy blanched. "I don't know what you're talking about."

Wolf's smile faded. "Okay, punk. You want to play games? We'll play *my* games."

His eyes riveted on Teddy, he snapped out orders to the other two men. "Chuck, take the woman in the other room and tie her up."

The broad-shouldered man in the leather jacket took a step toward Jennifer.

"Boone, keep that gun on the blind man." The hunched, older man moved in closer to Daniel, his gun wavering slightly.

Jennifer gasped as the man called "Chuck" dug his gun into her side. "Let's go, lady."

"Leave her alone!" As accurately as if he could see the

man's arm, Daniel struck out with one large hand and knocked the other man's gun free, sending it skating across the kitchen floor.

Furious, Arno hurled himself at Daniel, poised to slug him.

Jennifer screamed, and Boone moved in with his gun between Arno and Daniel. "Stop it, Chuck! He can't even see you!"

"That's enough!" Wolf shouted. "Get your gun, Chuck! And this time hold onto it."

He motioned Teddy against the wall with the others. "Get over there, Giordano." When Teddy hesitated, he shoved the gun against his ribs and growled, "*Now!*"

Teddy went to stand next to Daniel, whose face looked as if it had been carved from granite.

Wolf walked over to Daniel. "You don't look blind, mister," he snarled, "and you move pretty good for someone who can't see."

When Daniel remained stonily silent, Wolf turned his attention to Jennifer, his expression changing to a predatory stare that made her weak and sick with fear. Her breath lodged in the desert of her mouth, and she cringed, digging her hands into her sides until she nearly whimpered with the self-inflicted pain.

"You're the blind man's lady?" Again, the sly, paralyzing smile.

Unable to force a word out of her mouth, she nodded, trying desperately to look at something—anything—other than his face.

A pale, surprisingly smooth hand snaked out to capture her chin, forcing her to look at him. "His wife?"

Again she nodded, squeezing her eyes shut against the cold, bloodless touch of his skin against her face.

Unexpectedly, he dropped his hand. "Then I suggest," he

said softly, "that you convince him to be a good boy and do exactly what he's told. And I also suggest that you do the same."

Jennifer shuddered at the corruption she could almost feel flowing from the man. It seemed to seep through her own skin, freezing her blood. *He's insane,* her mind clamored. *He's insane . . . and . . . evil.*

Suddenly he seemed to lose interest in her, transferring his attention back to Teddy. "Where are the kids?" he barked.

Teddy didn't look at him. "Pittsburgh, I guess," he snarled.

Wolf sneered and slapped the younger man, hard, without warning. "I *said* . . . where are the kids?"

Glaring at him with undisguised fury, Teddy's answer was a stubborn, grim silence.

"You're making me very angry, Teddy-boy," Wolf said mildly. "I should think by now you'd know it's a mistake to make me angry." He glanced at Daniel, his mouth twisting to a derisive smile. "Now then, punk," he said, still watching Daniel's face, "you're going to tell me where the Angelini brats are, or I'm going to put a bullet between the blind man's eyes." With an ugly, teasing motion, he turned the gun on Daniel and mimed the act of shooting him.

Then he aimed the gun at Teddy, waiting.

A rope of perspiration banded Teddy's forehead. He looked from Wolf to Daniel, then back to the man with the gun. Finally, his voice ragged with defeat, he said, "They're upstairs." He moistened his lips and added hurriedly, "Wolf, leave them alone! Haven't they been through enough? They don't know anything—just leave them alone!"

Ignoring him, Wolf glanced at Boone. "Get upstairs," he ordered shortly. "Stay with those kids until I get there."

His gun still on Teddy, he half-turned to Arno. "Take her

out of here and tie her up." He inclined his head toward the doorway into the great room, adding, "In there. And watch her close." He smiled his chilling smile. "She looks like trouble to me."

Jennifer felt her face drain of color and her entire body begin to tremble when Arno jabbed her with the gun. "Come on, lady. Move it!"

"Jennifer—" Daniel lunged toward her, but stopped when Wolf pressed the tip of the gun barrel to his forehead.

"Sit down, blind man! Or I'm going to make your woman a widow!"

Jennifer stole one last look at Daniel's face, rigid and lined with frustration, as Arno and Boone prodded her out of the kitchen.

13

The great room that had earlier seemed so cozy to Jennifer now appeared eerie and forbidding in the flickering glow of the oil lamps and the dying embers in the fireplace.

Looking around the dimly lighted room, Arno muttered irritably, "Where's the upstairs in this—"

His words were lost in the sudden loud din from the stairway as Sunny came roaring down the steps, snarling and barking furiously. She was headed for Arno, as if she knew he represented the most critical threat at the moment.

Standing behind Jennifer, his gun shoved hard into her back, Arno jumped and yelled, instinctively turning the gun on the retriever.

"*No!*" Jennifer screamed, hurling herself in front of the dog. "Sunny—*no!*"

The dog thundered to a dead stop, all four legs stiff and poised as she looked at Jennifer with confusion. Her brown eyes, dark with distrust, flicked to Arno as if to measure his reaction to her low, distinctly menacing growl.

"Sunny . . ." With great effort, Jennifer kept her voice even and firm. "It's all right, Sunny." She turned to Arno. "Please, she's my husband's guide dog. Don't—"

A muffled sound from the top of the stairs made her whirl around.

"*Nicky!* Go back inside the bedroom!"

The boy was standing at the top of the steps, staring down at Jennifer and the two men. Behind him, just far enough out of the bedroom to be seen, stood Jason, holding onto

Stacey's hand. The little girl looked drowsy, but frightened.

"Boone?" Nicky set his glasses in place, straightening them on the bridge of his nose. His gaze went from Boone to Arno, lingering on the gun in the burly mobster's hand. "What are you guys doing here?" The boy's face was hard and unexpectedly mature.

"Hey—Nicky!" Grinning, Boone started toward the stairs but stopped when Sunny's growl increased to a warning snarl.

"Mommy?" Jason's voice sounded small and extremely uncertain. Leading Stacey along beside him, he moved a few steps closer to Nicky. Stacey rubbed at her eyes, staring down into the great room with dawning awareness. Seeing Arno holding a gun, her eyes widened, and her mouth formed a little bow of surprise.

Arno grabbed Jennifer's arm from behind, and pushed the gun into her back again. "Lady, you get that dog out of my way, or I'll blow her to bits!" he grated roughly.

Jennifer swallowed hard, looking wildly from the retriever to the children standing at the top of the steps.

I mustn't panic . . . oh, Lord, don't let me panic.

"Jason . . . " Her voice was tremulous. She stopped, then said again, "Jason, I want you to call Sunny. Then I want you children to go into the bedroom, shut the door, and stay there. With Sunny. Do you understand?"

The boy looked at her, then at Arno and Boone. "Where's Daddy?"

"He's in the kitchen with Teddy . . . and another man. He's all right, Jason. Now, please, honey—do as I say."

The boy's eyes went from Arno to Boone. "Who are *they?*"

Helplessly, Jennifer looked at Nicky.

Nicky's almost black, snapping eyes flicked from Arno to Boone. Glaring at the older man with disgust, he asked,

"Wolf's in the kitchen, right? With Teddy? You guys are here to finish what you started with Papa, I suppose."

Boone's face sagged with a wounded expression. "No, Nicky," he whined, shaking his head. "We just need to talk to you and Teddy. Teddy's got something that belongs to Mr. Sabas."

Nicky didn't take his eyes off the man as he said, quietly, "Jason, call Sunny now, like your mother told you."

Jason moved a few steps onto the landing, then stopped. "Sunny. Come on, girl!"

The retriever turned and looked up the stairs, then uncertainly back to Jennifer.

Again, Jason called her. This time, she hesitated only an instant before sprinting up the steps.

"Go back to the bedroom, Jason," Nicky told him. "Take Sunny and Stacey with you."

Responding to the tone of authority in Nicky's voice, Jason again glanced down the steps. When Jennifer gave him a small nod, he turned and led Stacey back to the bedroom. The retriever followed obediently.

"Get upstairs with those kids," Arno growled at Boone. "And *stay* up there with them, you understand?"

Boone hesitated, glancing from Arno up to Nicky. He put his gun away before starting to shuffle up the steps.

"Better keep your gun handy if you're coming up here to *guard* us, Boone," Nicky sneered, folding his arms across his chest. "An unarmed man wouldn't have a chance against three dangerous kids like us."

"Hey, come on, Nicky," Boone said peevishly, hauling himself up the stairs with noticeable effort. "You know old Boone wouldn't lay a hand on you or Stacey. We just want to talk to you, that's all."

Nicky pushed his glasses up with one finger, then leveled a scathing look of contempt at the man on the steps. "Talk about what, Boone? How you killed Papa? What you're going to do to Teddy . . . and to us?"

By the time he reached the landing, Boone was gasping for breath. "Now, you just hush that kind of talk, Nicky!" he muttered defensively, wheezing hard. "I told you, Teddy has something that belongs to Mr. Sabas. We just came to get it back. No one's gonna hurt you or your sister."

"Cut the gab and get those kids in the bedroom!" Arno bellowed from downstairs. "And *keep* them there, you hear?"

"Come on, Nicky. We'd better do like he says," Boone grumbled.

The boy glared at him with a mixture of anger and contempt. "Still letting Rambo rattle your chain, huh, Boone?"

"Nicky—" Boone glanced down at Arno with unease.

Ignoring him, Nicky looked down the steps at Jennifer. "Don't let him scare you, Mrs. Kaine," he said, glaring at Arno scornfully. "He thinks he's a real tough guy, but he doesn't have the backbone of a slug."

Arno scowled up at the boy but said nothing, waiting until Nicky and Boone finally disappeared into the bedroom before again jabbing his gun into Jennifer's ribs.

He forced her over to the couch, motioning curtly for her to sit down. Then, keeping his gun trained on her, he reached inside his jacket with his free hand and withdrew a twist of rope.

"You don't have to tie me up," Jennifer said, cringing at the tremor in her voice. "I'm not likely to make any trouble, not when someone has a gun on my husband and my son."

As if he hadn't heard her, he put the gun on the table beside the couch and snapped, "Put your hands behind your back."

When Jennifer hesitated, he shouted, "Lady, just *do* it!"

Not only did he bind her hands, but he trussed her ankles together as well. Straightening, he retrieved his gun and glanced around the dimly lighted room. "What kind of place is this, anyway?" he asked Jennifer. "You guys farmers or what?"

She shook her head. "It's a camp. For handicapped children," she said tonelessly.

His lip curled with distaste. "*Handicapped* kids? A camp for cripples?"

Jennifer stared at him incredulously, for an instant too angry and offended to reply. "They're not . . . *cripples!*" she finally managed to choke out. "They're children. Handicapped children."

He looked at her with disgust. "What's with you, anyway? You're married to a blind man, workin' in a camp for crippled kids—you got something against *normal* people?" He paused, moving in closer to her. "I bet there's something wrong with *you*, too, huh? Maybe something you try to keep a secret. Something that doesn't show, right?"

Another madman, she thought wildly. *And this one has the mindset of a Nazi.* She squeezed her eyes shut. He was so close she could hear the rasp of his breath, could smell some kind of sickeningly sweet hair grooming product, could feel his small, cold eyes on her.

Unexpectedly, he moved away and started walking around the room. "Who else is here besides you and your family? And Giordano and the kids. Anyone else?"

Jennifer hesitated, relieved that Gabe and Lyss weren't caught in this nightmare with them, yet half-wishing they were. Two more adults might have made a difference.

"I said, who else is here?" He stopped walking and scowled at her.

"No one." The words were lost in her choked-off panic, and she repeated them, forcing a note of calm into her voice.

"No one else. The couple who manages the camp are on vacation. We're just filling in for them while they're away."

"You got a phone here, don't you?" His gaze scanned the room, locking on the wall phone.

"It's . . . out of order," Jennifer told him. "The storm . . . "

"Yeah, it's a real monster, ain't it?"

Jennifer had a sudden, almost irrational desire to laugh. Here she was, feeling more and more like an inmate in a concentration camp; Jason was locked upstairs with some kind of aging thug; and Daniel—her throat closed with sick fear—Daniel was being held captive by a lunatic. All the while she was expected to carry on small talk with this . . . *gorilla?*

"How long have Giordano and the kids been here, anyway?"

She looked at him. "I . . . I'm not sure."

Again, he moved closer to her, assuming a chin up, shoulders back posture of aggression as he rolled the gun around his hand almost casually. "You're not real smart, are you, sweetheart? Whatta pair, a blind man and a dummy," he said scornfully. "You're a looker, though," he added, sounding almost surprised.

The heat in the room seemed to suddenly disappear, and Jennifer shivered.

"What's a classy chick like you doin' hooked up with a blind man?"

When she neither answered nor met his gaze, he moved even closer. As if to deliberately intimidate her, he kept the gun trained on her while with the other hand he lifted a heavy wave of her hair, then let it tumble slowly over his fingertips.

Jennifer flinched and twisted her head to one side.

He laughed. "Nervous, are you? Relax, sweetheart. It could be a very long night."

Jennifer felt a wave of nausea sweep through her as he looked at her for a moment, then put his gun down and shrugged out of his jacket. "Might as well get comfortable," he said with a sly grin, "as long as we're going to be here for awhile, right?"

Daniel's apprehension mounted as he listened to the two men at the kitchen table. Seated beside Teddy on the harvest bench for almost three hours, he could feel the tension in the younger man each time Wolf spoke.

"Stall as long as you like, Teddy-boy. I'm in no particular hurry to go back outside." He shifted on his chair and said insolently, "I'm going to get what I came for eventually, but we can play games for awhile longer, if you want."

"I'm not playing games, Wolf," Teddy said, his voice low and tight. "I told you, I don't have any notebook. And those kids know *nothing* about Nick's business. You know he always kept his family isolated from that part of his life. He even shut *me* out."

"Oh, I'm not concerned with what the kids might know about Nick's business, Teddy-boy. I'm only interested in what they know about Nick's *death.*"

When Teddy made no reply, Wolf went on. "You see, some people might get the wrong idea about who took Nick out. If they were to listen to the wrong stories, they might even think some of his friends had something to do with it."

Daniel heard him get up and take a few steps across the room.

"We don't want anyone thinking bad stuff about the Family, do we, Teddy-boy? If the kids have any information at all about who killed their old man, we need to know about it. Right?"

"I *told* you, the kids don't know anything!" Now it was

Teddy who shoved himself away from the table, jumping to his feet. "Don't you have any feelings at all, man? They're just kids!" He stopped. His voice was thick with emotion when he added hoarsely, "Kids without *parents*."

"Sit down, punk. I'll tell you when you can get up." Returning to the table, Wolf's tone was no longer insolent but hard. "I think maybe you don't understand how serious this is. This is important, Teddy-boy. It's *extremely* important." He paused, and when he went on, there was no mistaking the threat in his words. "To help you understand, maybe you should think on this: You're going to give me the notebook tonight."

When Teddy would have interrupted, Wolf thumped the table hard to stop him. "If you *don't*—" he paused, his tone softer but even more menacing "—if you don't, then I'm going to start playing *my* kind of games. With your blind friend here."

"Wolf—"

"Shut up, Teddy-boy." Wolf's tone was still deceptively quiet. "Better yet," he continued, "maybe what I'll do is make the blind man a *dead* man . . . and play games with his wife."

The words hung ominously between the men for only an instant before Daniel's pent-up rage exploded. In a stunning flash of movement, he pushed the table with both hands, jarring it loose from the bolts securing it to the floor.

Leaping to his feet, he roared, "You won't *touch* her!"

"Sit *down*, blind man!" Wolf shouted. "*Now!* I don't think you understand what's happening here. I'll do anything I please. You've go no control over it, mister, *I've* got control! Now sit down and shut up!"

Daniel heard the safety of the gun click only a second before Teddy grabbed his arm, trying to force him to the bench.

"Dan, do what he says!" Teddy pleaded. "He's just crazy enough to shoot you!"

Every fiber of his body felt coiled to its limit, stretched beyond endurance for a long, suspended moment. Then, like a man with the breath of life punched out of him, Daniel sank slowly, grudgingly, to the bench. A mixture of defeat and helplessness washed over him in one enormous, crushing wave.

Merciful Lord, don't let him touch Jennifer . . . don't let these animals hurt her.

He flinched with surprise when he heard Teddy tell Wolf, in a lame, shaky voice, "All right. I'll give you the notebook."

There was a long silence. Then Wolf spoke. "I thought you'd come around—once you understood how important it is to us, Teddy-boy."

"But it's not here," Teddy said quickly. "I hid it."

"Where?" Wolf snapped suspiciously.

"In one of the barns. At the other end of the camp."

Wolf softly rapped the butt of the gun on the table. "If you're lying to me, Teddy-boy," he said softly, "you won't get a second chance. I'll line you and everyone else in this cabin up against the wall and start playing firing squad. Do you understand me?"

"I'm not lying," Teddy answered woodenly.

"I hope not, kid." After another moment of silence, Wolf ordered, "All right. Just stay where you are, both of you. I'm going to talk to Arno a minute, right here in the doorway, and then we'll go get the notebook."

He stopped, sniffed once, then again. "Incidentally, blind man, the gun will be pointed at your head—so behave yourself."

Both Daniel and Teddy remained stonily quiet while the other men carried on a hurried conversation between the two rooms.

". . . I'm taking the blind man with us." Wolf's speech was fast now, his tone sharp and authoritative. Daniel had the distinct feeling that the man's next words were emphasized for his and Teddy's benefit. "You go up and tell Boone what's going on, and make sure he understands. If I'm not back here within an hour, have him take care of those kids." He paused. "And you take care of the woman."

Then he turned and snapped, "All right, Teddy-boy. Get a coat for yourself and the blind man."

"I need my dog if I'm going outside," Daniel said quietly, slipping into the fleece-lined bomber jacket Teddy handed him on his return.

Wolf uttered a sound of disgust. "Teddy-boy can be your guide dog, blind man! Now, *move!*" Without warning, he cracked Daniel across the back of the neck with the handle of the gun.

Daniel's knees buckled as a fireball of pain shot through him. He staggered and lunged forward, almost falling.

Teddy grabbed for his arm, steadying him as he led him through the outside door.

"For pete's sake, Wolf," he grated angrily, "he's *blind!*"

"He's going to be *dead* if the two of you don't get moving!"

"Come on, Dan. The sooner I give them what they want, the sooner they get out of your life."

"You know better than that," Daniel muttered.

"Listen, Dan—just do what he says," Teddy whispered desperately. "Whatever you do, don't get him any more riled than he already is."

Outside, the snow had tapered to little more than a fine mist. When Daniel slipped and stumbled over a rock, Teddy caught him. "Wolf, this is crazy—let him stay in the cabin!"

Wolf's only reply to Teddy's plea was to brutally jab the

gun into Daniel's lower back.

"Dan . . . " Teddy's whisper was even softer as he clutched Daniel's arm, trying to help him plow through the snow. "Dan . . . I know it doesn't help . . . but I'm sorry . . . I'm so sorry for what I've done to you and your family."

Too dazed by pain to even answer, Daniel could only nod his head.

14

Jason couldn't quite make up his mind about the man called "Boone." He didn't have the same . . . *bad* look in his eyes as the other two men did. Yet Nicky seemed to be really angry with him, apparently because of something to do with his "papa."

Jason had never heard anyone call their daddy "papa" before. Maybe that was the kind of word *geniuses* used. He had heard Teddy talking to Uncle Gabe and Daddy about Nicky, explaining how Nicky was a *genius*. Apparently, being a genius meant you were different from other kids, because Nicky also attended a special kind of school.

But right now, Jason thought Nicky looked just like any other kid who was upset with someone. He was frowning at the tall, thin man. His dark eyes snapped with anger, giving him a fierce look.

Still holding onto Stacey's hand, Jason listened to the conversation taking place between Nicky and Boone.

"I didn't have nothing to do with hurting your papa, Nicky. I wouldn't have laid a hand on Nick. No way."

Nicky pushed his glasses up a notch, staring up into Boone's craggy face. "I know that," he said impatiently. "It was Wolf. Wolf and Arno."

The man stiffened, taking a step back from the boy. "How'd you know that?"

Nicky didn't answer, but simply continued to watch Boone.

"Whatever you do, boy, don't let on to them that you know anything," Boone warned him in a gruff voice. "Now listen, Nicky, you tell me the truth. *Were* you in the house? Did you hear what went on the day your papa . . . the day he died?"

"Why do you want to know, Boone? Did Wolf tell you to shut Stacey and me up, too?"

Jason watched, fascinated, as the man swallowed. His neck was extremely long and skinny, with a pronounced lump at the base of it that rose and fell every time he swallowed or even took a deep breath.

"Nicky, honest now, I'm tellin' you the truth! The only reason we're here is to get that notebook that belongs to the Boss—Mr. Sabas—and to make sure you and Stacey get back home safe. Now that's all there is to it, and you're just gonna make trouble for you and your little sister if you don't do what Wolf tells you."

Nicky's only reply was a challenging sneer.

Boone glanced over his shoulder at the closed door, then moved closer to Nicky. He stooped down, lowering his voice as he said, "Listen to me, Nicky. If you—" his eyes went to Stacey for an instant, "—if you or your sister heard anything that went on at the house the day . . . your papa died, don't admit it."

Jason saw with surprise that Nicky's eyes had suddenly filled, as if he were about to cry.

"You were there that day, weren't you, Boone?" Nicky asked quietly. "You and Arno . . . and Wolf."

The man shook his head forcefully. "I wasn't! I swear to you, Nicky, I *wasn't!*" He looked away, then back to Nicky. "I was in the car. I didn't know anything until it was all over. Until Arno told me later. That's the truth, boy. That's the truth."

He straightened, coughed, and went on. "Your papa did something he shouldn't have done, Nicky. He tried to get the Boss—and the Family—in trouble." Again he shook his head. "He shouldn't have done that."

"So Wolf killed him," Nicky said flatly. "And now he's going to kill Teddy. And maybe Stacey and me, too."

"No!" Boone forced a weak laugh. "Why would he kill Teddy? Wolf likes Teddy, you know that. We *all* of us like Teddy!" He grinned at Nicky. "For a kid who's supposed to be so smart, you sure gotta lot of crazy ideas, you know that?"

Nicky stared up at him for a long time. The room was absolutely silent, except for Sunny's even, shallow breathing. Jason stood by her, confused by Nicky's argument with the man.

Finally, Nicky spoke. "*You* guys are the crazy ones, if you really think Teddy has that notebook." An odd little smile broke across his face as he watched Boone's reaction to his words.

"What?" The man's voice was gruff. "What do you mean?"

Still smiling, Nicky said, "I heard Arno talking to you out in the hall a few minutes ago. About Teddy and Wolf going to find the notebook." His dark eyes went over the man's face with a measuring look. "But *I'm* the one who hid the notebook, not Teddy."

Boone had straightened to his full height. Now he stooped down again, wincing with the abrupt movement. He grasped Nicky firmly by the shoulders and shook him slightly. "Don't you lie about this, boy!"

Sunny growled and took a step forward. Jason, too, moved forward, unsure what he could do, but wanting to help Nicky. Seeing them move, Boone quickly straightened again, holding up both hands, palms outward, as if to show that he meant no harm to Nicky.

Jason gave Sunny a quiet command to stay, and the dog settled beside him.

"What about the notebook, Nicky?" Boone asked,

keeping a cautious eye on the retriever.

"Do you think Papa would have trusted anyone but me with that notebook?" Nicky said softly, his eyes glinting with a strange expression.

Boone shook his head. "Then why did Teddy run off with you kids the way he did? And why did he tell Wolf what he did?"

"To protect us," the boy said, emphasizing each word as if he were the adult and Boone the child. "Teddy knows Wolf too well. He was trying to get him away from us."

Boone's eyes narrowed. "Are you tellin' me the truth, Nicky?"

The boy nodded, his gaze steady.

"What in the world is Wolf gonna do when he finds out Teddy lied to him?" Boone rubbed his beard and frowned.

Nicky's voice was hard when he answered. "Wolf's going to kill Teddy no matter what. We both know that." The two of them exchanged a look. Then Jason saw the same peculiar smile spread across Nicky's face. "Unless we stop him."

"Stop him?" Boone's chin trembled, but he looked interested.

Nicky's eyes lighted with sudden animation. "If I were to give *you* the notebook before Wolf finds out what Teddy's up to, do you think you could convince Wolf not to hurt Teddy—or us?"

Boone looked from Nicky to Stacey, moistening his lips. Finally, he nodded, and said, "Yeah. Sure." Again he nodded, more vigorously this time. "Sure, I could. Wolf would be so happy I got the notebook for him, he'd listen to me. Where is it?"

Nicky blinked, then said evenly, "It's not in *here,* Boone. I'm smarter than that." He nodded, and Jason thought he looked pleased. "It's someplace where no one but me is ever going to find that notebook."

Boone scratched his head.

"Listen, Boone, I'll take you to it. We'll get that notebook before Wolf can catch on to what Teddy's up to." He stopped, lowering his voice even more. "But you've got to promise me that you won't let Wolf or that creep, Arno, hurt us."

Boone put a hand on the boy's shoulder. "Hey, Nicky—you've got my word." He pressed his thin lips together in a worried expression. "But how are we gonna get the notebook? Chuck's right downstairs underneath us with the woman. And I'm supposed to stay with you kids 'til Wolf gets back."

Nicky pulled his mouth to one side and pushed his glasses up on his nose. "Hmm," he said thoughtfully. He looked at Jason and Stacey, then back up at Boone. "I know what we can do," he said decisively.

"What?"

"We'll just have to tell Arno the truth. Now, here's what we'll do, Boone. You go downstairs and explain to Arno about the notebook. Tell him where we're going, and that Jason and Stacey will have to stay with him. Then you and I will go after the notebook."

Boone cocked his head to one side, scratched his chin, then raked the back of his knuckles down one cheek. "Yeah," he said slowly. "Arno won't stop us, once he knows where we're goin'."

He glanced at Sunny. "I don't know about that dog, though." He gave Nicky a secretive grin and half-whispered, "He'd shoot me for sure if he knew I told anyone, but Chuck is scared to death of dogs."

Nicky laughed with him. "We'll take Sunny with us. Hey, she can even help us dig."

"No," Jason protested uneasily, beginning to feel angry with Nicky. "Sunny won't go with you unless I tell her to. And

I'm not going to tell her to. She's supposed to stay here with us." He suddenly felt very frightened. There was nothing familiar or safe in this room except Sunny.

When Boone knit his shaggy eyebrows together in a frown of displeasure, Jason stepped back but continued to stare stubbornly at the man.

"Now listen here, kid, we don't have time to waste. We're gonna go get that—"

"Wait a minute, Boone," Nicky interrupted, tugging at his sleeve. "You go on down and tell Arno what we're going to do. Let me talk to Jason a minute, okay? I need to explain all this to him and Stacey."

"Well . . . all right," Boone agreed after a long moment. "But the dog'll have to go with us, remember that. You get your coat on and be ready."

Nicky stood still, watching as Boone turned and shuffled stiffly out of the bedroom. He waited only an instant before hurrying across the room, his bare feet padding softly on the wooden floor. Quietly, he slid the bolt on the door.

Puzzled, Jason stared at him. "What are you doing?"

Nicky turned around, his back to the locked door. Putting a finger to his lips, he cautioned them to be quiet.

His eyes behind his glasses looked like black coals, sunken and shadowed against the pallor of his skin. Turning sideways, he placed his ear against the door, listening. Finally, he turned back to Jason and Stacey.

"Why did you lock him out?" Jason asked, bewildered by the other boy's behavior.

Nicky looked first at Jason, then at his sister. "I'm eliminating some of their ammunition," he said quietly.

"Huh?" Still confused, Jason frowned at him.

Nicky left the door and quickly crossed the room. "Wolf would have used *us* to get what he wanted from Teddy—or from your parents," he explained. "He wouldn't think twice about shooting all three of us if it would help him."

"How do you know so much about those men?"

"They work . . . for the same people Papa did," he answered shortly. "They used to be at our house a lot."

Jason knew he might not like the answer, but he had to ask the question. "They're not good men, are they?"

Nicky shook his head, taking Stacey's hand when she came to stand beside him. "No, they're not," he said bluntly. "Boone's probably the best of the three, but that's not saying much. Lucky for us, he's not too bright. The one downstairs—Chuck Arno—he's not a whole lot smarter than Boone, but he can get mean. He's kind of weird, you know? Thinks everything has to be perfect, or it's no good."

He stopped, glanced down at Stacey and, with one hand, distractedly squeezed her shoulder, earning a smile from her.

"Wolf is the dangerous one," he went on. "Wolf is smart. Maybe as smart as I am," he said matter-of-factly, with no hint of pride. "But my papa said once that Wolf's brain is probably rotten by now, from all the drugs he's done."

He hugged Stacey more tightly to his side. "Being around Wolf always makes me feel kind of . . . creepy. I think he likes to hurt people. I mean, really *likes* it." He shook his head. "Wolf's the worst of them, that's for sure."

"What are we going to do now?" Jason asked him uneasily.

Nicky didn't answer right away. His eyes scanned the room as if he were looking for something, finally coming to rest on the tall, narrow window beside the bed. "What's outside that window?"

Jason followed the direction of his gaze. "Just a porch." He tried to remember what Mommy called it. "A . . . balcony."

Nicky's eyes brightened. "A balcony?" He dropped his

hand from Stacey's shoulder and went quickly to the window. Without opening it, he peered outside for a long moment.

When he turned back to them, he was smiling.

15

Convincing Stacey to slide down the ice-glazed support post that ran from the balcony to the lower deck was almost as difficult as coaxing Sunny to jump.

Jason could understand Sunny's reluctance. She was a *dog*. But he didn't see why Stacey was making such a big deal of getting off the balcony.

Nicky had thrown a pillowcase of stuff over, and then Nicky and he had easily skimmed down ahead of her.

All three of them had hurriedly pulled on jeans and coats over their pajamas. Now, staring up at her from below, Jason almost laughed. Stacey, looking stuffed and awkward in her multi-layered outfit, seemed to find any kind of movement difficult.

Refusing to budge from the balcony, she glared down at her brother and Jason. "Let Sunny go first," she whispered a little too loudly.

"Shh!" Nicky warned her. "They'll hear us." He glanced around. "Jason, try to get Sunny to jump. Stacey won't stay up there by herself. If Sunny comes down, *she'll* come down."

But for the first time Jason could remember, Sunny refused to obey. Jason tried gesturing silently to her, as he had seen his daddy do any number of times, but Sunny continued to look down at him without moving.

Exasperated, Jason planted his legs apart, then spread his arms wide. He slipped in the snow and grabbed at Nicky to keep from falling. Opening his arms once more, he ordered as loudly as he dared, *"Sunny—come!"*

The retriever only cocked her head and stared down at him. "Sunny doesn't want to jump," Stacey announced gravely. "She wants to stay here with me."

Jason looked at Nicky for help.

He studied both the dog and his sister for a moment, then whispered harshly, "Stacey, throw Mrs. Whispers down to me."

Looking as horrified as if he'd asked her to set herself ablaze, Stacey crumpled her face, puffing her mouth into a circle of protest. "I *won't!*" she whispered back. Glaring down at him, she clutched the rag doll tightly against her.

With a soft groan, Nicky shut his eyes, obviously groping for patience. When he opened them again, he flashed a conciliatory smile and said more gently, "I'll catch her, Stacey, I promise. Just toss her down to me. Come on. You'll see why in a minute."

Stacey gave her brother one more look—a scrunched-up pout Jason thought of as a "mean look"—then carefully dropped her doll over the bannister. Both she and Sunny watched the descent of Mrs. Whispers into Nicky's arms, Sunny with curiosity, Stacey with fearful eyes.

As Nicky caught the doll, he said, "Now, Jason—call Sunny!" He looked up at his sister. "Stacey, help Sunny over the bannister. Hurry!"

It was obvious to Jason that Stacey no longer trusted her brother's judgment, but after a few seconds, she stepped behind the retriever. Jason again opened his arms and pleaded with Sunny to jump. The dog glanced questioningly from Jason to the doll in Nicky's arms, then darted a quick look over her back at Stacey. Finally, she raised herself as much as possible on her hind legs, thrust her head forward, and scrambled clumsily at the low-set bannister.

"*Now,* Stacey," Nicky rasped. "*Push!*"

Stacey squeezed her eyes almost shut, took a deep breath, and, screwing up her face into a terrible scowl, pushed at the retriever's back end until Sunny went over the edge with a yelp.

The dog hit both Jason and Nicky when she landed, sending them sprawling into a deep snowdrift. As Sunny stood over them, vigorously shaking off the snow that had splattered onto her coat when she landed, the tumbled boys looked at each other for a moment, then broke into a fit of muffled giggling.

Momentarily forgotten, an indignant Stacey stared down at them. Then, her eyes squeezed tightly shut and her lower lip tucked securely under her upper front teeth, she pushed herself over the railing and went sliding down the post to join the boys.

"Come on," Nicky said breathlessly, hauling himself up and pounding the snow off his coat. "We have to get away from here and go help Teddy and your dad."

He grabbed Stacey's hand, and the three of them with Sunny, hurried to hide just inside the row of snow-covered bushes that ringed the cabin.

"What about Mommy?" Jason whispered as they huddled down within the shrubbery.

Nicky looked at him. "You're right." He drew in a deep breath, then nodded decisively and said, "We have to get Boone and Arno out of the cabin."

"But how?"

Nicky pressed his lips tightly together, looking away as if he were watching for something in the distance. When he finally spoke, his voice was so soft Jason could barely hear him. He seemed to be talking to himself, as if he were thinking out loud. "When they realize we're gone, Arno's going to send Boone outside to look for us. If we can keep Boone from going back into the cabin, Arno will get uneasy and come out, too. He has your mom tied up, so he won't worry about leaving her alone for a few minutes."

He stopped, looking soberly at Jason. "We'll have to take care of Boone *and* Arno." A fleeting look of uneasiness crossed his features. "Then we'll go after Wolf."

Jason watched Nicky with wide, admiring eyes. Nicky was really smart, and he wished he could think even half as fast as the other boy. But did they really have any hopes of handling three grown-ups—grown-ups with *guns?*

"All of them?" he asked apprehensively. "How?"

"One at a time," Nicky assured him with confidence. "We can do it. Boone won't be any problem. Arno—" he shrugged, "—I'll just have to think of something when the time comes."

Jason didn't feel any better. "Why did you bring that stuff?" he questioned, pointing to an enormous bandana handkerchief Nicky had borrowed from him and the pale blue pillowcase he'd taken just before they escaped from the bedroom.

"You'll see," the other boy answered. "Stay down, now. We have to watch for Boone."

Kneeling down out of the wind, they waited. Within moments, they heard a furious pounding upstairs.

"That's Boone," Nicky whispered, "trying to get back into the bedroom."

Through the loft window, which they had left open, they could hear Boone banging on the bedroom door, shouting with surprised frustration. The uproar went on another two or three minutes, then ceased.

Shortly after that, they heard voices coming from the great room. Angry voices, but they couldn't hear the conversation.

Motioning for the other two children to stay where they were, Nicky crept out from the bushes and tiptoed up the steps onto the deck.

Jason and Stacey watched him press himself against the wall beside the window. He stayed there, listening to the muffled voices inside the room until they grew louder. Then he sprinted across the deck, bolting down the steps and back to the shrubbery just long enough to whisper, "Boone's coming out! I'm going to hide beside the steps. When he gets about halfway down, I'll trip him. As soon as you see him fall, come and help me."

"But what are we going to do, Nicky?" Jason asked.

Before turning to leave, Nicky touched his shoulder and grinned. "We'll take care of old Boone! Don't worry. Just trust me. Okay?"

Jason swallowed hard and nodded. Then Nicky was gone, running back to the cabin steps. He reached under his coat as he ran, yanking his belt off and rolling it up. When he got to the steps, he crawled into the bushes at the side, crouching down low so he couldn't be seen.

Within seconds, the door opened and Boone stepped cautiously out onto the deck, the snow crunching under his feet. Carrying his gun in one hand and gripping the bannister with the other, he trudged over to the steps, then started down.

Jason held his breath as he watched Boone plop his feet down, taking one step at a time and looking back and forth around the yard as he descended. He was only two steps away from the bottom when Nicky's hand snaked out and yanked his left foot out from under him.

With a startled cry, Boone went flying off the steps, landing face down in the snow. His gun sailed out of his hand and landed several feet away. At the same time, Nicky jumped out of the bushes and hurled himself onto the man's back. Taking their cue, Jason and Stacey ran to help, followed by an excited Sunny, who seemed to think it was all a game.

Boone was lying in the snow, apparently stunned. Nicky sat on his back, pulling Boone's arms behind him while he whispered frantically at Jason, "Help me tie him up! Hurry!"

Jason threw himself onto Boone, pressing his arms down as hard as he could while Nicky, still riding the man's back, pulled the pillowcase over his head.

As the boys struggled, Sunny pranced back and forth, kicking snow up into the air over Boone's body.

"Stacey—hold his head down!" Nicky commanded, jumping off Boone long enough to unroll his belt.

The girl frowned at her brother for only a second before flinging herself across the now struggling man's shoulders. Flattening herself and pushing down, she forced his head even deeper into the snow.

While Stacey and Jason held the mobster down, Nicky used his belt to bind Boone's hands behind his back.

Boone's protests were muffled by the pillowcase as Nicky started to pull him across the snow. "Come on, you guys—help me! We'll put him in that building beside the cabin!"

"The fruit cellar," Jason said, going around to the other side of Boone. While the boys half-pushed, half-pulled the stunned man across the yard to the fruit cellar, Stacey followed cheerfully along behind, talking softly to Sunny.

It was pitch black and cold as a tomb inside. They pushed the bound man up against one wall. At Nicky's instructions, Jason cautiously lifted the pillowcase up over Boone's head. At the same time, Nicky moved to tie and gag the man with the bandana handkerchief before he could utter more than a brief, furious grunt of protest.

Grabbing the pillowcase, Nicky went back outside, holding the door until Jason and Stacey came out. Then he secured it with a wooden crossbar.

Back at their original hiding place in the bushes, Jason

whispered, "What do we do now?"

Nicky looked at him. "Now we wait for Arno to come out."

16

Gabe stepped slowly down from the cab of the semi, waving his thanks to the driver who had given him a lift from town. The good-natured driver had offered to turn off the main highway and try his luck on the narrow country road leading in to the Farm, but Gabe had insisted he could walk the rest of the way. The man had already done enough; he didn't want him to risk the road into the Farm this late at night. Besides, Gabe knew he needed some time alone before he faced the others with the news of Lyss.

The road was heavily drifted, but the snow had stopped. Gabe thought the worst of the storm might be over as he trudged down the road toward the entrance gate, limping slightly. The ruts left by the Cherokee when he and Lyss had driven out were already more than half-covered. He began to watch for light from the main cabin as soon as he passed the weathered old barn and empty farmhouse that had once belonged to Yancey's Dairy. He was almost halfway down the road before the unlighted security lamps reminded him of the power outage.

As he plugged along the snow-covered road, he tried to think of something other than Lyss. But, as always, she had top priority in his thoughts. Even when he wasn't actively thinking about her, he was still fervently praying for her.

He had prayed all the way into town, watching her blood-soaked, lifeless form in the cab of the truck. Over and over, between supplications for Lyss, he thanked the Lord for the trucker who had come along no more than ten minutes after the accident.

After the young man had checked on them and the other driver, he had jumped back into the cab of his rig and used his CB radio to notify the hospital of the accident.

The genuinely concerned driver had taken Gabe and Lyss most of the way into Elkins, knowing the risk of moving her, yet afraid to wait for the ambulance which had met them halfway. Gabe had anxiously watched the quick transfer, and then sat helplessly while the medics worked in controlled urgency. Unbelievably, the semi driver had followed them to the hospital and stayed through the long hours with him. When Gabe was ready to leave the hospital, he offered to take Gabe back to the Farm. Gabe had been touched by the kindness of strangers before, but never in such an unselfish, significant way—and never when he had needed it more.

He had spent the first hour at the hospital in a near daze, praying silently but desperately the whole time the doctors checked his injuries. When they finished, he paced the deserted waiting room, stopping every few minutes to ask the admitting clerk if there was any word on Lyss yet.

By the time one of the Emergency Room doctors finally came to talk with him, he was almost incoherent with worry. His entire body trembled so violently, the doctor grasped him by the forearms to steady him.

"Mr. Denton, why don't you sit down?"

The doctor's abrupt suggestion sent a wild surge of panic roaring through him. "Lyss . . . she's not . . . "

"Your wife is still unconscious," the doctor said quickly. "It will be several hours before we have enough test results back to give you any kind of prognosis."

"But she's alive." His voice was weak with relief, but he resisted the doctor's attempt to lead him to a chair.

"Yes. But . . . "

"Can I see her? I have to see her—please."

"Perhaps in a few moments. She's being moved to intensive care. Someone will tell you when you can go in. But, please understand, Mr. Denton, that she won't know you're there. Your wife is in very serious condition."

He stopped, and Gabe was hit by another blitz of fear. Pressing his hand against the wall to steady himself, he was surprised to feel a touch on his shoulder, accompanied by a soft voice. "Take it easy, buddy. The Lord's in control of this, you know."

Gabe stared at the young truck driver; he had actually forgotten he was there. The man smiled at him, and for some reason this unexpected kindness nearly undid him. His eyes suddenly burned with scalding tears, and the trembling of his hands grew even more pronounced.

"Mr. Denton, are you sure you're all right?" the doctor asked, watching Gabe with concern. "Dr. Kline said your injuries were minor, but maybe we'd better have a closer look at you."

Gabe raised one hand, shaking his head. "No, I'm fine. I'm okay. Just . . . tell me about my wife. Please. I want to know how badly she's injured." His eyes caught the doctor's and held his gaze. "And I want the truth," he added quietly.

The pleasant-faced doctor nodded briefly, then gave him a thorough, cautious description of Lyss's condition. He explained that she had a number of external injuries—"a great many cuts, lacerations, and abrasions"—but that these were all "treatable."

Gabe soon realized, however, that the longer the doctor talked, the worse it sounded.

"Her right arm is broken, and she has a compound fracture in her right leg, as well." He stopped when he saw Gabe wince. "Those will cause her some pain and discomfort," he admitted, "but, again, they're treatable." He hesitated, studying Gabe as if wondering whether or not he dared continue.

Gabe saw the look. "What else?" he asked shakily.

The doctor sighed. "She has some fractured ribs, and I'm afraid that's creating a more serious problem."

Gabe pulled in a deep breath, waiting.

"One lung has been punctured. We've applied drainage tubes for now. We'll watch it closely and in a few more hours do further x-rays to see if the lung is re-expanding. If it is, she won't need surgery."

"Do you think it *will* . . . re-expand?"

The doctor shrugged and smiled ruefully. "It's too soon to tell. But I'm hopeful."

Gabe swallowed hard against the choking knot of anxiety in his throat. He could wait no longer to ask. "Her face . . . "

The doctor nodded, watching him carefully. "Yes," he said quietly, his eyes gentle with understanding. "She's going to need some reconstructive . . . and cosmetic surgery. But, again, Mr. Denton, let me emphasize that the injuries to her face are treatable." He paused. "I know it's difficult. But with time . . . " He left the thought unfinished.

Gabe looked away. Lovely Lyss . . . she had the face of a model. Perfect features, flawless bone structure, exquisite skin . . . .

Oh, Lord . . . just let her live . . . please . . . I'll help her through all the rest. I'll love her through it, Lord. Nothing matters except her life . . . please, Lord, in your mercy let her live.

Again he struggled for a deep breath. "She was unconscious . . . . " He began, then lost his voice to a tremor that shook his entire body.

The doctor frowned, measuring him as if he expected him

to fall over at any instant. He gave a small nod. "Yes, and she most likely will be for some time yet. She was in shock when you brought her in. Until I saw the x-rays, I thought she might have a ruptured spleen, but she doesn't. She has lost a lot of blood, however." He managed a tired smile. "We're working on all that, Mr. Denton. We'll do our best for her, I promise you."

Gabe searched the doctor's light gray eyes. "There's one thing I don't hear you saying."

The other man met his gaze. "You want to know if she's going to be all right."

Gabe waited, saying nothing, unable to breathe.

The doctor hesitated. "I can't give you any guarantees. But you asked me for the truth, and I *am* trying to give you that. Your wife is in critical condition. She has sustained some life-threatening injuries. Bringing her here promptly gave her a fighting chance. Waiting any longer could have killed her. Now we're going to do everything we can to help her make it, and right now I feel that we have her pretty well stabilized. But I can't promise you anything. Not yet."

Gabe pressed a fist against his mouth to choke off a sob. He squeezed his eyes shut for a moment, then opened them, ignoring the tears that threatened to spill over. "Thank you . . . for leveling with me."

He pulled in a long ragged breath, then abruptly asked, "The driver of the truck that hit us—how is he?"

The doctor's face brightened a little. "He's going to be just fine. He has a concussion and a broken collar bone, but he's doing nicely."

Gabe nodded. "That's good," he said softly. "Lyss will be glad for that. It wasn't his fault, you know. The road . . . " His words fell away.

No, it wasn't the truck driver's fault. The blame belonged to someone else. The little mafia hood who sucked all of us into this nightmare . . . he's the one responsible for Lyss being where she is . . . .

He shook his head, trying to banish the roaring hammer of anger that had begun to pound at his mind. "Please," he said thickly, "may I see her now?"

They allowed him only a brief moment with Lyss before insisting that he leave. He knew he would carry with him for the rest of his life the memory of that first look at her in the cold silence of the hospital room. Nothing could have prepared him for the sight of her, lying there as still as death, tubes everywhere and all of them connected to some part of her body. Casts and splints and bandages . . . so many bandages, especially on her face.

He couldn't see her face for all the bindings, and for just an instant he felt a shameful pang of relief. He *had* seen it, in the headlights of the truck. And he would see it again and again, he thought, for years to come. It had been photographed by his mind in one stark, agonizing second and was now an indelible part of his memory. He would never forget the wave of abject terror that had seized him, shaking him and pushing him to the very edge of insanity before something deep inside his soul had cried out the reminder that the face still belonged to Lyss . . . this was Lyss, his wife, his lovely, beloved Lyss . . . .

After his brief time with her in the hospital room, he had gone in search of the doctor to tell him he would be leaving for awhile, explaining that there was something he had to do that wouldn't wait. The doctor encouraged him to go, reminding him he wouldn't be able to see Lyss again until late the next morning.

Before Gabe left the hospital, he remembered to call the number Teddy had given him. He reached the same man with whom Teddy had spoken earlier. Impatient and rushed, he told him about the power outage, the hazardous road conditions, and the accident, describing the limousine they had been following just before they were hit by the semi.

The voice at the other end of the line had promised to get someone on the way as soon as possible, warning, however, that Virginia was also suffering the effects of the same snowstorm. The weather might cause a significant delay in getting anyone there. Angry at the thought of delay and desperate to get back to the Farm, Gabe stopped at the nurse's station and asked an aide to call the police.

"Tell them to come out to Helping Hand Farm as fast as possible," he said hurriedly.

The aide lifted the telephone receiver, then paused. "I'll call, sir, but I don't know how much good it will do. We've had two other major accidents within the last hour and a bad fire on the south side." She shrugged helplessly. "We're a small town—"

"Look, just *try,*" Gabe pleaded, his head beginning to throb harder than ever. "Maybe the state police would help—just call *someone!*"

When the aide had shrugged again helplessly, Gabe had stormed out of the hospital.

Now, as he finally crossed the yard and headed toward the cabin, Gabe shivered, not from the cold, but from the impact of all that had happened during this long night. He suddenly felt extremely tired, exhausted physically and emotionally. But the night wasn't over. An even heavier weight of dread settled around his heart as he realized that, thanks to Teddy Giordano, this night might *never* be over.

His head began pounding again as he paused at the steps to the deck. He took a deep breath and waited for the throbbing to subside. Something above him, something . . .

out of place . . . caught his attention. His eyes scanned the front of the cabin, the deck, the windows, then the second floor—

"Uncle Gabe!"

He heard the loud whisper at the same time his eye caught the open window upstairs. He whirled around, looking first at Jason, who stood tugging urgently at his coat, then again at the gaping window where a white curtain billowed in and out.

"Jason?" He stared at the boy, then glanced at the retriever standing expectantly beside him. "What in the world are you doing out here?"

Jason grabbed his hand. His eyes were wide and excited—too excited, Gabe thought. The boy looked terrified.

"Uncle Gabe! You've got to help!"

Jason began tugging almost violently on his hand, and it suddenly occurred to Gabe that the boy was close to hysteria.

Quickly, he enfolded the small hand between both of his and squatted down to put himself at Jason's level. "What's wrong, cub? What is it?"

"The men! The bad men are here!"

Gabe saw that he was trembling, saw the glint of fear in his eyes, and felt himself turn cold with apprehension.

"The bad men?"

Jason nodded fiercely. He tried to explain, but his whispered words ran together in a white heat of desperation. Gabe's head began to swim with bewilderment.

In the end, it was Nicky who made him understand. Seeing Jason with his uncle, he and Stacey shot out of the shrubbery and came running up to Gabe, drawing him closer to their hiding place.

Nicky, too, was breathless and excited, but far more

coherent than Jason. He told Gabe their incredible story quickly but clearly. Beginning with the arrival of the three men, he ended with their capture and detention of Boone.

"You put him *where?*" Gabe gasped with amazement as the recital ended.

"In the fruit cellar," Nicky replied matter-of-factly. "Then we came back here to hide until we could figure out how to get rid of Arno."

"Arno . . . "

"The man inside with Mrs. Kaine," Nicky reminded him.

Gabe's mind was spinning. Still somewhat dazed and disoriented from the accident, he found it difficult, if not impossible, to take in everything the boy was telling him. If only his head would stop pounding.

Gabe rubbed a hand over his eyes. "So you told this . . . Boone . . . that *you* hid the notebook. This is the notebook Teddy's supposed to deliver to the federal marshal?"

"Yes, sir. My papa's notebook."

"Well . . . *did* you? Hide it?" Unreasonably, Gabe found the boy's unflappable manner infuriating.

Nicky met his gaze for an instant, then turned to Jason. "Jason, the way Sunny's prancing, why don't you and Stacey take her over there beside the tree?"

Jason glanced down at Sunny. The retriever was circling him restlessly, pawing at the snow-covered ground. "You have to go, Sunny? Come on, girl." He took Stacey by the hand, and the two of them followed the dog off to the side of the cabin.

As soon as they were out of earshot, Nicky looked up at Gabe and said, "The notebook is inside Stacey's doll—Mrs. Whispers."

Dumbfounded, Gabe could do nothing but stare at him. When he finally found his voice, it cracked with disbelief. *"You put it in your sister's doll?"*

"I didn't," Nicky said evenly. "Papa did. Before . . . they killed him."

In spite of the cold, Gabe felt a wide band of perspiration pop out on his forehead. "Stacey doesn't know?"

Nicky looked at him with mild disdain. "Of course not. She doesn't *need* to know. She's as careful with that doll as if it were a real baby. Papa knew where the notebook would be safest."

Gabe shook his head, trying to clear his mind, trying to get a grip on what was left of his sanity. *These people weren't real . . . real people didn't live this way.*

Abruptly, he glanced at the cabin. A figure moved, silhouetted against the window from the glow of an oil lamp. The figure stopped, moved again, then disappeared from view.

Before Gabe could muster a rational thought, much less an answer, Jason and Stacey returned, with Sunny prancing at their side.

"Mr. Denton?"

Gabe stared at Nicky in the darkness.

"I think we better see about Arno first. Wolf told him if he wasn't back in an hour, Arno was to—" he faltered, looking at Jason, "—he was to shoot Mrs. Kaine."

Gabe's throat closed. "Jennifer?" he mouthed softly. "Would he—would he do that?"

The boy nodded solemnly, looking at Gabe as if he were surprised he'd even ask. "Yes, sir. He would. And once Wolf realizes that Teddy lied to him—" He stopped, but his gaze never wavered. "Wolf is insane. He'll kill anyone who crosses him," he added softly.

"Uncle Gabe?"

Gabe turned to look at Jason.

"Where's Aunt Lyss?"

"She's . . . in the hospital, Jason. There was an accident."

The boy's eyes widened. "Aunt Lyss got hurt?"

Gabe moistened his lips, cracked almost painfully from the cold and the dryness of his fear. "Yes. A truck hit the Cherokee, not long after we left. Your Aunt Lyss . . . was badly injured."

Jason's lower lip trembled. "But she'll get better?"

"I—hope so, Jason." He thought he couldn't take much more. He felt as if he had been hurled full-force into the middle of a nightmare that had no end.

He suddenly became aware of a gentle but persistent tug on his coat sleeve, then his hand. Glancing down, he met the dark-eyed gaze of a sober-faced Stacey. "I'll ask Jesus to make her well."

Unable to answer her, he managed to squeeze her hand before he looked away, struggling to gain control of his teetering emotions.

"What are we going to do, Uncle Gabe?" Jason's whisper was choked and thready. "How can we get Daddy and Mommy—and Teddy—away from these men?"

Gabe lifted an unsteady hand, taking another few seconds before turning back to the children.

He glanced around wildly. What should he do? Storm the cabin with three kids and a guide dog? For a moment, he had an almost hysterical urge to laugh. What should he *do?* That was rich. What *could* he do?

"Mr. Denton?"

Nicky's voice was soft, little more than a guarded whisper.

Gabe looked at him irritably. The kid had grated on him

from the beginning, at first because of what Lyss had called his *precociousness*. Now, however, he looked at him and saw an extension of Teddy Giordano. It was unfair. It was immature. It was probably even un-Christian. But at this moment, he could barely stand the sight of Nicky Angelini. Because of him, his precious Lyss was hovering near death.

His response was curt, even gruff, but the boy simply looked at him with that steady, older-than-time wisdom. His dark, unreadable gaze appeared to register Gabe's dislike, even understand it.

"Sir? I think I may have an idea."

17

When Arno heard the moaning, he first thought it was the wind. Even when it grew louder and more insistent, he merely wondered if the storm had picked up again.

It was the dog's barking that made him go to the window and look out. He glanced back at the woman, who was staring at the window with startled eyes.

"Is that the guide dog?" he asked her gruffly.

She hesitated, then nodded. "It sounds like Sunny, yes."

"Then Boone must've found the kids." Seeing nothing, he turned and left the window, coming to stand in front of the woman.

"Oughta teach those kids a lesson, pullin' a stunt like that," he growled, staring accusingly at her.

He didn't like the way she was staring back at him. Who did she think she was, anyway? *She* was the one mixed up with a bunch of defects, not him. She needed to be taken down a notch or two, like most women. Once Boone got the kids back inside, he'd settle her dust, teach her how to show a little respect around a real man.

He jumped, startled when the dog began to bark more wildly. The low moaning now sounded closer, louder.

"What the—"

It was coming from the front of the cabin. He walked slowly to the door that opened from the great room onto the deck. The top half of the door was glass, but the louvered shutters were closed, making it impossible to see out.

Cautiously, Arno opened one of the shutters and stared

out into the black night. The window was fogged, but even when he cleared it, there was nothing.

The eerie keening started again, louder than ever, once more accompanied by the barking dog.

He swallowed hard, glancing back at the woman. She was staring at him with that hollow-eyed, contemptuous look that made him want to take a swing at her.

He shifted the gun to his left hand and opened the opposite shutter, but he still could see nothing except the thick, snow-veiled darkness, a darkness that could hide anything.

It was the sound of his own name drifting in off the wind that finally snapped his control.

"Chhuckkk . . . "

His blood froze. It had to be Boone! He must be hurt. But how?

Suddenly, the dog stopped barking. There was nothing but snow-filled silence.

He released his breath, at the same time tightening his grip on the gun.

Then it came again. *"Chhuckk . . . help meee . . . "*

He jumped violently, his heart lurching to a violent stop against his rib cage. He poised, transferring the gun back to his right hand as he stared warily at the door. Slowly, he reached for the doorknob, turned it a little, then more. When the lock released, he cracked the door, then opened it an inch at a time.

He stood in the doorway, looking and listening. There was nothing. Nothing but darkness and that mind-chilling moaning.

After turning to look back at the woman once, he moved forward, stepping over the threshhold and onto the deck, the gun extended outward from his body. He waited, took one more step, and froze.

"Help meee . . ."

His head whipped to the right, and he choked out a cry of panic as the guide dog came roaring around the side of the cabin at full speed. Her head was low, her mouth open in a furious, snarling rage as she raced toward him. The ground seemed to tilt under him, and Arno felt his bones turn to butter. The gun in his hand began to shake violently.

Terrified, he shouted. A palsied trembling shook him as the vicious-looking dog reached the bottom of the steps—and stopped. Stopped on command.

Before he could even grab a breath, a heavy, boot-clad foot came swinging up from somewhere beside him, cracking his wrist in a painful blow, sending his gun flying out of his hand, out across the steps and into the snow-laden bushes.

He whirled, raising his arm to strike out too late. A blond-haired man in a blue ski jacket whacked him with a high kick and a straight-line punch, knocking the wind from him.

Arno reeled, fell backward against the wall of the cabin. Again he struck out, blindly this time, twisting, kicking, clawing in panic as he wheezed for air.

The man came at him again, and Arno felt his blood turn to ice when he saw the rictus of pure rage on the guy's face. He saw the punch coming, and scrambled to duck it, but suddenly lights went off in his head, and the night erupted in blinding white flashes.

Two fleeting thoughts knifed through the pain as he went down. Out of the corner of his eye, he saw the dog turn and go running like a crazy thing, away from the cabin and out into the field, and he felt a stroke of insane relief at its leaving.

Then, seeing the incredible fury on the face of the man who had attacked him, he wondered who the guy was and why he was so crazy-mad.

Jennifer saw most of the scene between Gabe and Arno through the open door. She watched with dazed astonishment as her brother-in-law efficiently knocked the thickset mobster unconscious, then bound his hands with a length of clothesline from the storage pantry.

By the time Gabe, Jason, and the Angelini children came to untie her, she was on the verge of screaming with relief. Instead, she began to sob, losing the last thin shred of her self-control.

She made two or three attempts to pull herself together while Gabe worked on the rope, but once he had freed her hands and feet, she could no longer restrain the wave of agonizing terror that had held her captive throughout the evening. When Jason threw his arms around her and Stacey came to touch her face, Jennifer cried even harder. Stacey, seeing Jennifer weep, started crying with her. Nicky, however, walked away, going to the other side of the room to stand quietly and watch them.

Still on his knees beside her, Gabe tossed the rope aside and clasped her shoulders. "Jenn—are you all right?"

She nodded weakly, wiping her tear-stained face with the back of one hand. "Yes . . . I'm . . . " She tried to tell him about Daniel, but her lips were trembling so fiercely she couldn't make him understand.

"Jennifer . . . take it easy," he soothed her, still gripping her shoulders firmly. "It's okay now. You're all right."

She shook her head violently, finally forcing out the words. "*Daniel!* He's out there, with that awful man, that—*Wolf.* He took Daniel and Teddy . . . and he has a gun . . . " She began to shake, her entire body giving into the horror of the past few hours.

Jason backed off a little, glancing at his uncle with frightened eyes. Gabe quickly reassured him with a small nod, grasping Jennifer's shoulders even more tightly. His own voice was none too steady when he spoke. "Jenn, I need to go after Dan. You've got to pull yourself together, so I can leave the kids with you." He watched her. "Jenn?"

She nodded, hearing him, trying to do as he asked. Struggling for control, she pulled in deep breaths, hugging her arms tightly to her body. Gabe dropped his hands away from her shoulders, and she squeezed her eyes shut once, hard, then opened them as she felt her head begin to clear.

Gabe straightened and helped her get awkwardly to her feet. "I'm . . . I'm all right," she told him. As she stood, she rubbed her wrists where the rope had burned her skin.

He watched her carefully as if he were afraid she would collapse at any moment. "Sure?"

Again she nodded. Then, looking at Jason, she exclaimed, "Where *were* you? They said you went out the bedroom window. I was *terrified!*" She stopped. "The man who was outside looking for you, where—"

"Jennifer," Gabe's voice broke off her questioning, and she turned to him. For the first time since he had come running into the room, she saw how awful he looked. His face was scratched—or was it cut? There was a small bandage by his ear. His eyes were deeply shadowed and bloodshot, and he looked positively stricken.

Suddenly, a thought hit her, and she asked, "Where's Lyss?" Her eyes scanned the room as if she expected to see her sister-in-law standing there.

When he didn't answer, she looked at him more closely and said again, "Gabe? Where's Lyss?"

She caught her breath when he turned his anguish-filled eyes on her and said, "She's in the hospital."

Too stunned to say anything, she could only stare at him, waiting for him to explain.

Quickly he told her about the accident, the doctor's description of Lyss's injuries—and the questionable prognosis.

When he had finished, Jennifer searched his pain-seared face for a glint of hope. Seeing none, she looked away, staring mutely into the distance.

Would this nightmare never end? The children held hostage, Lyss critically injured, Daniel . . .

Daniel!

She whirled around to Gabe, but he was already moving toward the door. "As soon as I'm out that door, you bolt it behind me," he told her, his voice now surprisingly strong. He even managed a weak attempt at a smile when he told her, "I'll let the kids fill you in on what they've been up to since they went out the window."

"Gabe, be careful . . ."

"You just stay put," he said grimly. "I'll be all right." Again, he started to the door.

Nicky's voice stopped him. "Mr. Denton?"

He turned, frowning.

"Arno's gun," the boy reminded him. "Shouldn't you take it with you?"

Gabe looked at him. A muscle in his jaw clenched, and his mouth turned hard. "Not everybody settles their problems with a gun," he said bitterly.

Jennifer's hand went to her mouth. "Gabe, maybe you should . . ."

His eyes were flinty. "I've never had a gun in my hand, and I don't intend to start now."

"Would you let me go with you, Mr. Denton?" Nicky pressed. "I know Wolf, how his mind works . . ."

"That's where you're wrong, kid," Gabe snapped. "Creeps like your mob pals—their minds don't work at all. They live by instinct. *Animal* instinct." He paused. "Thanks, but I'll take my chances alone."

As Gabe went out the door, Jennifer's gaze went to Nicky. The boy looked as if he had been struck.

Suddenly, she realized something else. Turning to Jason, she exclaimed, "Sunny! Where is she?"

The boy hesitated. "She went to Daddy," he answered quietly, his face sober. "I told her to go help Daddy."

Jennifer slid the bolt on the door with a trembling hand, praying with all her heart that Sunny and Gabe wouldn't be too late.

18

Standing near the wall of the barn, Daniel heard Wolf's voice thicken with menace.

"Punk! You lied to me, didn't you?" His tone was soft, but every word was oiled with warning.

Teddy's reply bounded down from overhead. "Hey, man, I was nervous! And it was dark. But I hid it in this hayloft, so it's got to be here."

Listening intently, Daniel thought he could almost touch the electric tension between the two men.

"Oh, you were nervous," Wolf sneered. "Teddy-boy, I'm disappointed in you. It's not like you don't know better. You worked for Nick long enough to learn *some* smarts, didn't you?"

When Teddy didn't answer, Wolf went on, his words falling quietly off his tongue with a sinister smoothness. "For sure, you got to know me and the Family well enough to learn you don't play games with us. Right, punk?"

"I'm not playing games! This *is* where I hid the notebook. It was dark, and I was in a hurry. You're just going to have to give me a little time, that's all." There was an edge of desperation in Teddy's voice, his words shooting out fast and sharp, like jagged pieces of glass.

"Get down here, punk!"

Daniel stiffened at the change in Wolf's tone. The snide, almost playful note of banter was gone, exchanged for a malevolent hiss of anger, an anger that sounded increasingly explosive.

"Hey, Wolf, chill out, huh?" Uneasily, Daniel heard the change in Teddy's voice, too. His brash assurance seemed to have fled. In its place was a distinct thread of fear. "Listen, man, if you'd just take that gun off me, it would help. You're makin' me so nervous I can't even think. Give me a break."

"Shut up, punk! Just—*shut up!*" The mobster's voice was now a shrill, almost feminine shriek. "I'm not wasting any more time with you! We'll let those smart-mouthed Angelini brats dig up the notebook!"

Daniel flinched when he heard a sudden movement from the hayloft. If Teddy panicked and tried to jump this maniac, he wouldn't have a chance.

"I told you, the kids don't know where it is! They don't know anything about it, Wolf. Leave them alone!"

"We'll see, punk. We'll see."

"Wolf, will you be reasonable—"

Daniel heard a click. The gun. He took a cautious step toward Wolf, judging his distance from the mobster to be only a few inches, no more than a yard. "Give him a chance," he said quietly. "You haven't even given him time to look."

"Dan, don't!" Teddy warned.

Ignoring him, Daniel took another step. "Put the gun on me," he said evenly. "Let him look however long it takes. No man can think with a gun pointed at him."

The only sound in the barn for the next long moment was the rasp of agitated breathing. His own, Daniel knew, as well as that of the other two men.

Suddenly, Wolf laughed. The brittle, humorless cackle made Daniel feel as if an icy blast of wind had howled through the building.

"What's this?" Wolf jeered, abruptly sobering. "You looking to be a hero, blind man? Huh? You want to play games, too, is that it?"

Suddenly, Wolf's arm slammed hard around Daniel's throat in a vicious grip. At the same time, he pounded the gun roughly into his back.

Daniel choked and bent backward, struggling for breath.

He sucked in air to ease the pressure on his windpipe.

"Sure, blind man! Have it your way!" Again Wolf laughed. "Hey, punk—your buddy here wants to die in your place! Which one of you wants to go first, huh? You or your pal?"

Daniel tried to think. He had already judged the mobster to be at least a head shorter than him. Even with Wolf's arm around his throat and a gun in his back, if he were quick enough, he thought he could swing forward and take him with him, roll him over his back, shake the gun free...

Then he heard Teddy shout, heard him move, and suddenly knew there was no time. He was going to jump.

Daniel twisted, trying to break free of the headlock.

He heard Teddy cry, *"Nooo!"* as he hurled himself from the loft. With one furious surge of strength, Daniel wrenched himself free of Wolf's arm, turned, threw himself at the mobster to throw off his aim. The gun went off, and he heard Teddy utter a small, odd sound of surprise as he hit the ground. At the same instant, the grayness Daniel lived with every day of his life suddenly exploded into a brilliant blaze of flashing colors. He went down, and the lightshow fizzled and faded to black.

The retriever stopped in the open doorway of the barn, watching the man who stood over her master with a gun. A low, primeval growl started at the back of her throat, and the man turned to meet her stare.

His own eyes were wild, opaque, and unfocused. He looked from the dog to the two men sprawled at his feet, then slowly returned his gaze to the dog.

With a muffled exclamation, he began to back away, his maniacal gaze still fixed on the retriever.

The dog's snarling grew louder, more threatening, and she took a step forward, into the barn. Still growling, she looked from the man backing away from her to the two men lying on the ground, her eyes locking on the larger of the two. If she were aware of the man edging backward toward the open door at the end of the building, she gave no sign.

She padded cautiously into the barn, the grinding noise in her throat now silent as she moved toward the two bodies sprawled on the ground.

Stopping beside the large, dark-bearded man first, she began nuzzling his face, then his shoulder, trying to coax a response from him.

She paid no further attention to the man with the gun who turned and fled the barn.

19

Through a gray haze of pain, Teddy watched Sunny as she nuzzled Daniel's shoulder, then began to lick his face. She whimpered softly a couple of times. Once she looked up, toward the far end of the barn.

Glancing at Teddy and seeing his eyes open, she transferred her attention to him, padding over to his side and pulling gently at his coat with her teeth.

He lifted a weak hand to touch the retriever, then turned his head to scan the barn. Seeing no sign of Wolf, he raised up off the ground, moaning with the effort.

He sat up, looking over his body, expecting to see blood. There was none. He rubbed his arms, his head, his neck. Surprised and relieved, he accepted the fact that he hadn't been shot. Then he looked at Daniel.

Feeling something pull in his back when he moved, he pushed himself up to his knees, wincing and catching his breath with the effort. His upper left arm was on fire with pain. Finally, he forced himself to crawl over to Daniel.

Sunny walked beside him, going again to stand by Daniel. Gently, she touched her nose to the side of his face, but he lay silent and unmoving.

"Dan?"

Teddy quickly examined the big man's body, his gaze locking on the wet stickiness seeping from his upper arm. He stared at him in horror, trying to think of some kind of first aid for a bullet wound.

Suddenly, Daniel stirred, groaning as he opened his eyes. He turned his head slightly. Lifting a hand first to his throat, then to his shoulder, he yanked it away with surprise when he touched the wetness on his sleeve.

"Dan . . . just lie still." Teddy breathed a shaky sigh of relief. "You took a hit in your arm. How do you feel?"

Daniel scowled and uttered another groan of pain. "My shoulder?"

"Yeah. I need to find something to tie it off until we can get you out of here."

"Wolf . . ."

"He's gone. I don't know where. We'll have to be careful, in case he's nearby."

Sunny began to whimper and lick Daniel's face excitedly. As he lifted his hand to stroke her ears, his frown was questioning. "Sunny? Where'd you come from, girl?"

The retriever burrowed her nose into the side of his neck for a moment, then sat down beside him, giving Teddy an expectant look.

"Are you all right?" Daniel asked Teddy dully. "Did he hit you, too?"

"No," Teddy answered quietly, studying Daniel's face. "Thanks to you, he didn't. I think I may have a dislocated shoulder and a sprained back, but no bullet holes."

Daniel gave a small nod, then mumbled thickly, "I should have a clean handkerchief in my pocket." He tried to lift himself up enough to get to the pocket of his jeans. "Help me wrap it around my arm, will you?"

Carefully, Teddy helped him free his arm from the sleeve of his jacket and wrap the handkerchief around his shoulder.

"You okay?" he asked, watching Daniel uneasily as he helped him back into his coat.

Daniel moistened his lips and nodded, propping himself against the wall of the barn.

Teddy searched the other man's face for a long moment. "Why'd you do a crazy thing like that, anyway?" he asked

abruptly. "He might have killed you!"
"Instinct," Daniel muttered.
Still watching him, Teddy said softly, "I don't think so. You were trying to save my life. Weren't you?"
Daniel tried to smile, but it was more a grimace. "Had to buy you some time," he said cryptically.
Teddy frowned. "What are you talking about?"
Daniel sighed, then coughed and rubbed his throat. "You don't want to die yet, Teddy," he said simply. "Not until you're ready for heaven."
Teddy thought for an instant that the man might be delirious, but a careful look at the expression on Daniel's face indicated that he was entirely lucid. He swallowed hard but said nothing.
Daniel let his head loll back weakly against the wall, stroking Sunny's ears with his good hand. "We can talk about that later if you want. Right now, we've got to get out of here, get back to the cabin." Suddenly more alert, he leaned forward. "Wolf—that's where he'll go, isn't it? The cabin?"
"Probably."
"We have to stop him." Daniel started to drag himself to his feet.
"He's still got the gun, Dan," Teddy said glumly, moving to help him. He slumped slightly under the weight as Daniel leaned against him.
"But he's pretty well fried. Whatever he's on, it's done a real number on him. I think the two of us can take him." He added tightly, "And it has to be before he gets back to the cabin. We might handle one at a time, but not all three of them together."
Teddy surveyed their surroundings, his gaze stopping on the big red Massey-Ferguson tractor parked in the middle of the barn. He studied it a moment, then turned back to Daniel. "That tractor. Does it drive pretty much like a car?"

Daniel considered his question, then nodded. "They're not hard to drive. Not if it's the MF. Gabe said Mac had left it in the barn."

"Yeah. You think I could drive it?"

"I used to drive one every summer when I worked up here for Uncle Jake. If I could drive one, I'm sure you can. Why?"

"I don't suppose the keys would be in it?"

"The keys?" Daniel shrugged. "Probably are. I doubt if Mac ever worries much about anyone stealing his tractor out here. But what are you—"

"Even if they're not, maybe I can hot-wire it," Teddy said, mostly to himself. He glanced sheepishly at Daniel who had lifted one dark brow knowingly. "Let's go for a ride, Dan."

"Are you sure you're able to drive?"

Teddy again braced himself for Daniel's weight, and the two of them moved slowly toward the tractor. "I don't know how far I'd get on foot," he replied. "My back feels like someone did a stress test on my spinal cord. But I think I can still drive. Maybe we can chase Wolf down before he gets to the cabin."

Daniel staggered then steadied himself against Teddy.

"You all right?" Teddy darted a worried look at him.

Daniel rubbed his throat and nodded.

"You may have to tell me how to start this thing," Teddy said as they started walking again. On Daniel's other side, Sunny instinctively began to herd her master in the right direction. Even though she wasn't on her working harness, she expertly blocked his legs with her body when he almost ran into a milk pail.

"Good, Sunny, that's my girl," Daniel automatically praised the retriever.

The keys were in the tractor's ignition. Excitedly, Teddy said, "All right! Let's go get him!"

He climbed up to the tractor seat, Daniel following to stand beside him.

"What about Sunny?" Teddy asked, looking down at the retriever.

Bracing himself against the fender, Daniel gave a short nod of his head. Sunny backed off a little, then came at a run and jumped up onto the steps of the tractor, squirming into a tight space beside Teddy's foot.

Teddy grinned at the dog, then turned to study the instrument panel. "Okay. What do I do first?"

Daniel thought a minute. "Push in your clutch. There should be a switch around the middle of the panel, maybe a little to the left. That's your fuel shut-off switch. Push it in. Then put it in neutral and turn the key."

"That simple, huh?" Teddy glanced over at him doubtfully.

"Let's hope."

Teddy rolled his tongue inside his cheek, took a deep breath, and followed Daniel's directions. When he turned the key over, he was afraid it wasn't going to catch, but after a couple of seconds, the tractor roared to life.

"Whoa," he said with a soft whistle. "How many horses are in this thing?"

"A bunch," Daniel said. "You ready?"

"What now?"

"Put it in gear and give it some fuel. There's a throttle on the floor. Then let your clutch out and go."

"Right," Teddy said under his breath. Finally the tractor lurched, chugged and went forward. "Here goes! Hey, Dan—has this thing got any lights on it?"

"Below the steering wheel. A little to the right. You've got work lights and flashers. You can run them separately or together."

"I want it all."

"Then turn the switch to the right as far as it will go."

Teddy turned the switch. "All *right!* We've got lotsa lights! Hey, this is a pretty tough machine. What's the attachment on the back? Looks like some kind of a motor with a metal pipe."

"Must be the PTO—the power take-off. That's your power machine to drive other equipment," Daniel explained, shifting a little to steady himself. "Mac was probably using it for the grinder-mixer, to grind feed for the cows. You want to stay well away from one of those if it's running," he cautioned. "It'll eat a man alive within seconds."

They left the barn, lights flashing. Teddy was impressed. Then another thought struck him. "Is the snow going to be a problem with this thing?"

Daniel shook his head. "City boys," he said with a small grin. "No, the snow won't be a problem. You're driving a four-wheel drive. It'll go through just about anything."

"Good thing. We've got some pretty spectacular snow-drifts out here."

It was surprisingly bright, even without a moon or stars. The entire field was a blanket of glaring whiteness.

"See anything?" Daniel asked anxiously.

Teddy shook his head, then caught himself. "Nothing yet. Hang on, I'm going to turn and head toward the cabin." He was surprised at how easy it was to turn the big machine around and start it in the other direction. They moved slowly around the side of the barn toward the field and the quarter of a mile that led to the main cabin.

In other circumstances, Teddy thought he would probably enjoy this. He liked to drive—*loved* to drive—and he had driven just about every kind of machine on wheels. He had even tried a semi a couple of times, but gave it up when he realized he would need a lot more training in order to be good at it. He liked the feel of the big MF under him, its solid strength, the sound of its power. He even got a childish kick out of the flashing lights. *Yeah,* he decided, *this could be kind of fun if it weren't for . . .*

Wolf! He was a hundred, maybe a hundred and fifty yards ahead, off to the right. Teddy saw him turn, stopping to stare at the tractor bumping across the field.

"There he is," he said softly to Daniel. "And you were right. He's headed toward the main cabin."

"Does he see us?"

"Oh, yeah," Teddy murmured as he continued to eye the mobster. "But I don't think he was *expecting* us."

At his side, Sunny sat up alertly and began to bark.

Surprisingly, Wolf remained where he was. Unmoving in the snow, he watched their approach as if he were too stunned to move.

They closed the distance by several more feet, the tractor roaring like an angry lion over the retriever's frenzied barking.

Then Teddy saw Wolf aim the gun. "Get down, Dan! He's going to shoot!"

Daniel ducked down as best he could, his hand snaking out to Sunny's head, holding her still. "Watch yourself!" he yelled at Teddy.

Not answering, Teddy continued to grip the wheel, arrowing in on Wolf with iron determination.

The mobster fired the gun once, then began to run, awkwardly. Teddy gave a grim little smile of satisfaction when he saw that it was impossible for the man to make any real headway in the snow. The field was layered with one enormous drift after another, and Wolf obviously wasn't wearing boots. For every step he managed to clear, he stumbled two or three more.

The tractor was closing the distance fast, and Wolf stopped running again, taking time to aim and fire.

"Stay down, Dan!" Teddy shouted without turning to look. "He's close enough to hit us now."

The mobster fired once, missed, and fired again, more wildly than the first time. He shouted something at Teddy, then turned and ran.

Out of the corner of his eye, Teddy saw that Daniel was having a hard time crouching down, and even more difficulty restraining the retriever. Apparently, the combination of the tractor noise and gunshots had agitated the dog. She twisted under Daniel's hand, barking and snarling angrily.

"Sunny, *no!*" Daniel ordered sharply. The dog quieted her barking but continued to pitch feverishly back and forth.

Closing in on the running man, Teddy could now see him clearly. Without coming to a halt, Wolf pivoted, aimed the gun, and fired. Seeing that he'd missed again, he fired once more, this time stopping for a better aim.

The bullet sailed by Teddy's head, close enough that he was sure he felt it split the air as it went by. But it missed, and he did a mental count on Wolf's ammunition.

Counting the shot that had wounded Daniel, Wolf's gun should now be empty. He decided to make sure.

He stood up from the tractor seat and yelled, "Hey, Wolf—wanna ride?"

He was close enough to see the mobster's furious, wind-burned face as he turned and raised the gun. Teddy ducked when the man aimed and fired, but nothing happened. The gun was empty.

Releasing a sharp breath of relief, Teddy lowered himself to the seat. He gripped the wheel with a look of unswerving purpose, heading straight for the man in the snow.

Wolf threw his now useless gun away and began to hurtle as best he could through the snow, looking wildly over his shoulder every few seconds.

"You can get up now, Dan. He's running on empty,"

Teddy said tersely, his hands glued to the wheel.

Daniel hauled himself up, removing his hand from Sunny's back as he did. Apparently, that was the chance she had been waiting for. Before Daniel even realized what was happening, the dog squirmed out of her cramped area and jumped from the tractor. Pounding across the remaining few feet of snow between her and Wolf, she barked fiercely as she ran.

"Sunny!" Daniel looked as if he were about to jump after her, and Teddy reached to hold him back, still keeping his eyes on Wolf. "She's all right, man! Stay put until I stop this thing!" He looked at the panel. "How *do* I stop this thing?"

Finding the brake pedal, he pressed it with his foot, bringing the tractor to a gradual stop. He took it out of gear, but let the motor idle. "Stay put, Dan. I'm going after Wolf!"

Without hesitating, he dropped to the snow-covered ground, ignoring the sudden roar that surged to life when he jumped. He bolted for Wolf, who was still running as hard as he could.

Sunny beat him there. She charged the mobster, leaped high in the air, and jumped Wolf's back, a golden fireball of fierce, high-powered fury.

"Way to go, *Sunny!*" Teddy yelled, adding his own weight to the retriever's as he, too, jumped Wolf. The mobster flailed his arms, groping, lashing out at nothing. Then he screamed and went down, hard.

20

Gabe saw the trio from across the field. Running with surprising agility in his heavy hiking boots, he cleared a snow-covered tree stump and went on, watching with amazement as Sunny hit the mobster.

He cried out a shout of encouragement to the dog, felt a thrill of grudging relief when he saw Teddy jump to help. Running as hard as he could, he watched Wolf go down, admitting to himself that Teddy was surprisingly good with his punches. One efficient chop and the mobster's hands stopped grabbing air and fell limply to his sides.

He was only yards away from the scene when he became aware of another noise, a noise that corroded his stomach with horror. The loud burst of power roaring from the PTO . . . Sunny or Teddy must have hit the lever when they jumped from the tractor.

He stopped dead for an instant, his eyes going to Dan. From somewhere deep inside him a blast of fear exploded and came gushing upward. He saw Dan jump from the tractor, then weave unsteadily as his feet hit the ground.

Gabe took off running, pushing himself, forcing himself so hard he was almost flying over the snow. The cold stung his face and burned his eyes as he ran. He kept his panic-stricken eyes fixed on Dan, who at first stood quietly unmoving, as if to get his bearings. Suddenly he stepped backward, the movement taking him an inch too close to the rapidly turning, grinding PTO shaft.

Gabe tried to scream, thought he had, then realized his terrified, desperate shout was still in his mind. Finally, he got it out. His chest pounding and burning, his heart banged painfully against his rib cage as he stretched his legs and continued to fly.

"Daann! Don't move! Dan . . . the PTO!"

Dan froze but too late. Gabe saw the bottom of his jacket touch the uncovered shaft. Over 500 rpms grabbed the material and started to wrap the coat.

Gabe's last warning was one long, unbroken scream of agonized terror as he watched Dan throw up a hand to grab something—anything. The movement only made him stumble even closer to the grinding power machine that was pulling him into certain death with furious, relentless speed.

With dreadful clarity, Gabe saw that he would never reach his friend in time. Dan cried out, a terrible sound of helplessness.

Gabe pushed himself to the absolute limit, knowing his chest was about to explode. He was close now, close enough to reach out with both hands to Dan when Teddy suddenly hurled himself at the trapped blind man. The force of his weight ripped Dan free of the PTO with sudden fierceness as he offered himself up to the machine like some kind of pagan sacrifice.

Gabe moved to grab Teddy, saw that the sleeve of his jacket was too far into the machine to get him free, then remembered the switch by the tractor seat. Throwing himself against the side of the tractor, he half-climbed, half jumped, hit the lever hard and pushed it back—

It stopped. Stopped just before it would have ground Teddy's arm to the bone.

Even though the tractor was still running, the sudden drop in noise was a relief as the PTO came to a stop, and Sunny, who had deserted the unconscious Wolf to go to Dan, stopped barking.

Gabe moved to kill the motor of the tractor, then ran to Teddy who was lying on the ground, bleeding but alive. He dropped down beside him and saw that he was unconscious. Tearing his ski jacket from his shoulders, he draped it over Teddy, then started toward Dan.

Shaking, but otherwise all right, Dan had already hauled himself up from where he had fallen after being knocked free of the PTO. He stood, not moving for a moment as he listened. "Gabe?"

Gabe reached for him, grasping his forearm. "Are you all right?" he choked out, his voice roughened by the tears lodged in his throat. Dan nodded, and after only an instant's hesitation, the two men embraced each other fiercely.

When Dan stepped back, Gabe still held him at arm's length. "Teddy?" Dan questioned. "Is he—"

"Unconscious. The shaft caught his arm. He's losing a lot of blood." He led Dan over to where Teddy was lying. "We need to get him out of here, to a hospital, but—"

"Jennifer!"

Dan suddenly seized Gabe by the shoulders, a look of dread settling over his features. "Where is she? Is she all right?"

"Jennifer's fine, buddy," Gabe reassured him. "Everything's under control—" He stopped, knowing he had to tell Dan about Lyss, but realizing that now wasn't the time.

"Thank you, Lord," Dan murmured shakily, dropping his hands away from Gabe's shoulders. "We've got to get an ambulance for Teddy, somehow, now," Dan said urgently. "But how—"

He stopped. Both men stiffened as they heard a whirring noise growing louder.

For a moment neither spoke as the thrumming sound of an engine grew gradually louder.

Gabe looked up. "A helicopter!" he exclaimed, seeing the

approaching lights in the night sky above them. "The federal people from Virginia! It has to be them!"

In his excitement, he grabbed Dan's injured shoulder, realizing what he had done when Dan flinched. "Ah, Dan, I'm sorry."

Dan made a weak dismissing motion with his hand. "I'm okay. Do they see us?"

"I can't tell yet."

"Do you think they can land in this much snow?"

"It's heavy enough to be packed pretty solid. The best place would be down by the gate, where I plowed earlier." Lightly, he pressed Dan's good arm. "Stay here—I'm going to turn on the tractor lights so they don't miss us!"

Teddy's hoarse whisper stopped him. "Gabe?"

Startled, Gabe froze, staring down at him.

Teddy's face was pale and pinched, his eyes barely open. "Thank you . . . for what you did."

Gabe looked at him, saying nothing. He wasn't angry anymore. He was simply exhausted. Exhausted and sick at heart. He felt nothing for Teddy Giordano, and was relieved by the utter lack of feeling. He hadn't the strength to feel. He was empty, drained, his spirit a desert.

Silent, Gabe tore his eyes away from the man on the blood-soaked snow. Running to the tractor, he climbed up, and switched on the headlights and flashers. Then he began to jump up and down, waving his arms and yelling. "Down here! *Hey! Here!* Here we are!"

The helicopter dropped low, hovering long enough for Gabe to see the pilot wave one hand in acknowledgment.

"They see us, Dan!" he yelled. Then, thinking fast, he made a pointing motion with one hand in the direction of the plowed lane leading to the gate.

The chopper came a little lower, circled, and headed in the direction Gabe had indicated.

Putting the MF in gear, Gabe started forward. "I'll be back!" he yelled to Dan. "I'm going down to the gate with the tractor. The lights will help guide them in!"

He bumped across the snow in the tractor, mumbling a hurried prayer of thanks as he went. When he reached the gate, he jumped from the tractor, leaving the lights on full and the engine idling.

The helicopter hovered, veered a little to the right, then began to descend. Gabe continued to pray. He didn't know how much traction one of those things had on snow—or on ice. What if it couldn't land?

But the chopper was down. It landed rough and hard—but safely. He could have cried with relief.

Both the pilot and his passenger jumped from the cockpit and ran toward him. Gabe practically fell on top of the pilot in his feverish excitement.

Words exploded from him in an incoherent spray as he tried to tell them everything at once.

The pilot took him by the arm, while the other man, the one in the suit and topcoat, moved to Gabe's other side.

"Mr. Denton? You *are* Mr. Denton?" The man in the suit had a quiet, soothing voice that finally penetrated Gabe's agitation. "I'm Keith—we talked on the phone." He reached for Gabe's hand and shook it firmly. "Why don't you fill us in on what's been happening so far, sir?"

Gabe looked at him incredulously. Suddenly, the scene in which he found himself took on an edge of absurdity. *Hysteria, Denton. You're headed straight for the twilight zone. You crack up now and these guys may just hop back into their whirlybird and go home. Come on, motor-mouth. The man wants to know what's been happening around here this evening. If there's one thing you can still do, it's talk.*

"Mr. Denton?" Keith again. "Are you able to talk with us, sir?"

Gabe squared his shoulders and took a deep breath. Then, like the professional newscaster he was, he began a brief, concise, and surprisingly unemotional report of the past few hours' events.

Driving the tractor back across the field toward Teddy and Dan, Gabe's mouth felt like toasted cotton. Using those few minutes, he explained to Keith how the kids had taken care of Boone, then recited a sketchy account of his own run-in with Arno. He described the scene he had witnessed between Teddy and Wolf—including how Teddy had saved Dan's life at the risk of his own. He ended his monologue by revealing the hiding place of Nick Angelini's notebook in Stacey's doll.

"And good luck on getting that doll away from her," he told the marshal with a dry smile. "You'd better figure out a way to get the notebook out of the doll without . . . *wounding* Mrs. Whispers, or you're going to have a major conflict on your hands."

As soon as Keith and the pilot began to work on Teddy, administering first aid and getting him secured onto a stretcher, Gabe told Dan about the accident . . . and Lyss. Doing his best to be reassuring, he answered Dan's questions as well as he could. The whole time he talked, however, he wished he *felt* as optimistic as he was trying to sound for Dan's benefit.

When they finished with Teddy, Keith and the pilot tied up Wolf—who was just beginning to regain consciousness. Loading Teddy, Dan, and Wolf on the tractor, Gabe took off slowly back toward the helicopter, Keith and the pilot staying abreast of them on foot. When they reached the chopper, Keith secured Wolf inside, then headed into the main cabin to check on Jennifer and the kids, and to make sure the other two mobsters were still down.

Gabe remained outside, with the others, waiting for the sound of a second helicopter. A large transport chopper, scheduled to take off only half an hour after the first one, should be arriving at any moment.

"Back-up," the marshal had explained earlier, while they were in the field. "I wasn't sure what we'd find here, after our phone conversation. It's a good thing I asked for it. With the three Sabas soldiers and the rest of you, we're going to need all the space we can get."

The pilot was keeping an eye on Wolf and setting off flares for the incoming helicopter. Gabe now stood by himself, leaning against the tractor just a few feet away from Dan and Teddy.

Dan was balanced on his knees in the snow, close to Teddy's stretcher, the faithful Sunny close beside him. Watching them, Gabe frowned with concern. He didn't think Dan looked much better than the man on the stretcher at the moment. He was pale and perspiring, even in the cold air. And he was rubbing his injured shoulder constantly.

Teddy had come to again only moments before, at least enough that he was attempting to carry on a feeble conversation with Dan. His face was pale and pinched, but he clutched Dan's hand and tried to speak in a weak, faltering voice.

Gabe didn't especially want to hear anything Teddy Giordano had to say, but he was too tired to move, so he stayed where he was, listening.

"Dan . . . you were right . . . "

"Right about what, Teddy?" Dan leaned closer to him.

"Both of you . . . you and Gabe . . . both of you put your lives . . . on the line for me tonight." He gasped, then choked out, "Remember, Dan? I said no one would do that for . . . someone like me." His grip on Dan's hand tightened.

Dan nodded. "But you did the same thing, Teddy—for me. I owe you my life."

Teddy attempted a weak grin. "Yeah, but you're . . . a good man, Daniel. A good man is worth . . . a little pain."

Gabe's eyes burned. Irritably, he wiped the back of his hand across them. The little mobster had that much right, anyway. A man like Dan was worth a *lot* of pain.

Dan's voice was almost as soft as Teddy's when he answered, and Gabe had to strain to hear. "What you have to remember, Teddy, is that in the eyes of Jesus, we're *all* worth a great deal of pain. That's what the cross was all about." He paused, then went on. "It was God's way of showing each one of us just how very special we are to Him. God loves you every bit as much as He does me—or Gabe. The cross was for you, too, Teddy. Not just for a few people who measure up. It was for all of us."

Gabe swallowed hard. He was sure Dan knew he was listening. And he was sure that last remark had been meant as much for him as for Teddy. Even blind, Dan could still read his feelings. He had known all along how Teddy had grated on him, right from the beginning, even before the accident and Lyss's injury.

Gabe squeezed his eyes shut, then opened them, knowing he had to face the truth.

He had seen the stranger in their midst as just that: a stranger . . . a potential threat to his self-satisfied world.

Teddy wasn't a part of their family. He wasn't even a Christian. He was a criminal. He was trouble. He was an outsider.

Sick at heart, Gabe realized he had forgotten what Dan had just told Teddy—that the Lord didn't offer His love and His forgiveness and His gift of eternal life only to those who measured up. He also offered it to the Teddy Giordanos of the world.

With a sorrowing, heavy spirit he remembered Nicky, the way the boy had looked at him when he rejected his offer of help, back at the cabin. *Even a child, Lord... I even rejected a child... and all because he's an innocent part of something I see as evil. Oh, Lord, forgive me... the syndicate is corrupt... but not that child.*

His heart seemed to stop as he heard a voice, somewhere within himself, say, *"Teddy's my child, too, Gabe... suffer the children... let them come to me... lead them to me, Gabe."*

An awareness rose in the back of his mind, a reminder that, had it not been for the Kaine family, Gabe Denton might well have been one of the Teddy Giordanos or the Nicky Angelinis of the world. *Or... even a Wolf or an Arno.*

Dan's parents—and their children—had taken the unhappy boy, Gabe Denton, into their homes and into their hearts. They had loved him and accepted him and given him a haven from his bitter, alcoholic mother who only wanted him to stay out of her way. They had taken him to church with their own family week after week for all those lonely years and taught him, mostly by example, about the all-inclusive, unconditional love of Jesus Christ. Had they not *suffered the child,* Gabe Denton might never have *become* a child—a child of the King.

Dazed by the flood of realization, he glanced down at Teddy, only dimly aware of the conversation still taking place between him and Dan.

"Dan, if I come out of this, I want—I *need* to talk with you about the cross. And about... some other stuff I read in Jennifer's Bible. Can we talk about that, Dan?" His whisper was growing weaker, his eyes fluttering, but he continued to grip Dan's hand almost desperately.

Dan moved even closer to him. "You bet we will, Teddy. We'll talk all you want. There's something I want to talk with *you* about, too." A smile broke across his haggard features. "I want to talk with you about a job, Teddy. A job on a farm."

Teddy's eyes widened slightly. He tried to speak but was too weak by now to get the words out.

"You know, Teddy," Dan said quietly, "a farm is a great place to raise kids. Maybe we can talk about that, too. When you're stronger."

Slowly, Gabe pushed away from the side of the tractor and closed the distance between himself and the two men on the ground. Tears spilled out from his eyes, blurring his vision, but he didn't care. He saw Dan give a little nod, as if he'd been expecting him, just before he knelt down beside him and Teddy, who was no longer conscious.

Gabe touched Dan lightly on the shoulder as he dropped to his knees, then took Teddy's hand and enfolded it between his own and Dan's.

"Keith's bringing Jennifer and the kids out to us," he said, his eyes tracing the strong, sensitive profile of his friend beside him. "You want to pray for Lyss . . . and for Teddy . . . while we're waiting?"

Dan smiled in his direction. Then they prayed together.

Epilogue

Helping Hand Farm *August*

"The Camp has turned out to be even more of a success than you dreamed it would, hasn't it, Daniel?" Jennifer asked quietly.

He nodded contentedly and squeezed her hand. They were sitting in the porch swing on the deck of the main cabin. Holding hands, they were simply enjoying the uncommon quiet of the evening and trying to catch their second wind before vespers.

This was "their Sunday" at the Camp. Every third week, Daniel, Jennifer, and Jason drove up to be a part of the Sunday worship and fellowship activities. Daniel usually offered the morning message for the campers' worship, and both he and Jennifer would lead the musical praise service for evening vespers. During the afternoon hours, they shared in the children's picnic and games, usually having as much, if not more, fun than the campers.

"It still doesn't feel right, not having Lyss and Gabe with us on Sundays." Jennifer's voice was touched by sadness, and Daniel draped an arm around her shoulders to pull her closer.

"Next year," Daniel said confidently. "Next year things will be a little more normal for all of us again. What with the trial and everything else . . . " Daniel let the sentence trail off, rubbing his arm absentmindedly.

Jennifer noticed and said softly, "It's hard to believe that one little notebook will destroy a crime ring. Wolf, Arno, and

Boone's trial will be next month. But I imagine the investigation will go on for quite awhile."

Daniel nodded, and they sat in silence for a few moments, swinging gently back and forth, lulled by the evening's sultry warmth and the sounds of the day gently winding down. They could hear creek water lapping at the rocks along the bank, and the crickets were already tuning up in anticipation of a long summer evening chorus. Every now and then a child would laugh or a dog would bark, but mostly the camp had settled.

Sunny dozed at Daniel's feet. Jason and the Angelini children had kept her busy most of the afternoon. Sunny's visits were always a treat for Nicky and Stacey. The three children were off just now with Teddy, helping to collect wood for tonight's bonfire.

Jennifer leaned her head against Daniel's shoulder, sighing when he pressed a gentle kiss onto the top of her head.

"I'm getting nervous about seeing Lyss tomorrow," she told him, turning to look up at his face. "Oh, Daniel—I don't know how she's endured all this surgery!"

His expression betrayed his own concern for Lyss. "Hopefully, the worst is over now. Gabe said from here on, the rest should be easy."

"If only this last surgery is a success. She's had those bandages on for such a long time, and she's so hopeful." Her tone softened even more when she added, "I think she's also scared. But, then, who wouldn't be? If I'm this apprehensive about the outcome, what must *Lyss* be feeling?"

"Lyss will be fine. She's said all along that if the Lord could take care of one face for her, He could handle the second one, too." He shook his head. "That's faith."

"She's been wonderful. She *is* wonderful."

Smiling faintly, he nodded his agreement. "Poor Gabe.

When all this first started, he was going to be so strong for Lyss. He was going to get her through it, remember?"

She burrowed her head more snugly against his shoulder, thinking out loud, "Mm. Lyss told me last week he's given the word *hover* a whole new meaning."

"I can imagine." Daniel laughed softly. "When we stopped over there Friday morning, she was threatening to lock him in the garage for the weekend."

Jennifer yawned, tempted to give in to the wave of drowsiness stealing over her, but unwilling to face the rude awakening that would come all too soon. "I think Stacey is really enjoying her birthday," she said groggily. "She loved her cornshuck doll. Naturally, she gave me to understand that it would have to share her affections with Mrs. Whispers."

Daniel laughed again. "She's a doll baby herself." He paused. "I hope we have a little girl someday. I think I could do a really good job of spoiling a little girl."

"You're already doing a fine job with your little boy," she said dryly. "Nicky and Stacey are both thriving on their new life, aren't they, Daniel? I've never seen two happier children. Teddy is just great with them."

"He's great with *all* the kids. Mac told me again today he doesn't know what he'd do without him. He says Teddy has more energy and works harder than any man he's ever known. And he says the kids absolutely adore him. Coming from Mac," he added meaningfully, "that's quite a tribute."

She nodded to herself. "It's sad that Nicky and Stacey's aunt didn't want to be bothered with them. She doesn't know what she gave up."

"That's true," Daniel agreed, "but I've got a hunch the children are better off. This would be a great place to grow up in, and between the MacGregors and Teddy, they'll have all the love and attention they need."

"They'll be starting school soon. I hope they adjust all right. Going to a small rural school is going to be awfully different for them, especially for Nicky after that private, accelerated school for the gifted he was in."

"He'll probably be filling in as a substitute teacher by the end of the first quarter," Daniel said with a grin. "Wonder what that boy's going to be when he grows up? A nuclear physicist or a space lab designer?"

"As a matter of fact," a voice said behind them, "he's decided to be a farmer."

"Teddy!" Jennifer jumped, startled. "You're still as quiet as a cat!"

"Nicky wants to be a *farmer?*" Daniel asked with amusement.

"Yep," Teddy said, coming around the swing to perch on the wide bannister. "The entire future of agriculture has new hope."

Teddy had changed, too, Jennifer thought. His arm had healed without any permanent damage, and he had gained some weight—not too much, but enough to make him look a little healthier.

He looked happy, too. He no longer appeared so tense and *hunted.* Now his eyes held a perpetual twinkle—along with the familiar glint of mischief—and he was seldom without a smile.

"Everything going all right?" Daniel asked him.

"Everything's good," Teddy replied, smiling at Jennifer. "I'll never be able to thank you enough for giving me a chance at this job, Daniel. I like it so much, I almost feel guilty taking a salary for it."

"That could be a real problem, Teddy," Daniel said gravely, "since Mac's dead set on your getting a raise next month."

Teddy grinned. "I can always donate it to charity."

Jennifer decided right then she was going to have to shop around for a girl for Teddy. She would certainly have no problem recommending him to any of the young women in their church family. He was nice looking, intelligent, amusing, brave. Any man willing to take on two children like Nicky and Stacey as a single parent had to be *extremely* brave, not to mention the way he had saved Daniel's life. That, of course, was what would endear Teddy Giordano to her for always.

On the more practical side, he was a hard worker, and he had a good, steady job. Best of all, he was now an enthusiastic Christian, thanks to Daniel's and Gabe's interest and involvement in his life. Yes, she decided, not realizing that she was staring at Teddy with a somewhat conniving smile, she'd definitely have to do some girl-shopping on his behalf.

Teddy looked at her curiously, started to say something, then glanced across the field at the road. "Someone's coming."

Jennifer leaned forward to look. "That's Gabe's T-Bird!" She jumped up from the swing and walked to the end of the deck. "Daniel—I think Lyss is with him!"

By the time Gabe pulled in and parked on the turnaround across from the cabin, Jennifer, Daniel, and Teddy were waiting in the yard.

"Daniel, Lyss *is* with him!" Jennifer exclaimed eagerly, clutching his arm as she watched Gabe go around to open the door on the passenger's side.

After allowing Gabe to help her from the car, Lyss turned to face Jennifer and the others. She was wearing a pink floral sundress and had scooped her hair to one side with a pink silk scarf.

"The bandages! The bandages are off, Daniel!"

Beside her, Daniel's voice reminded Jennifer that he was

waiting for information about his sister. "Does she look . . . very different?" he asked, his voice low and tense.

"I can't tell yet." Jennifer started walking, hesitantly at first, then more quickly, clasping Daniel's arm to guide him, since he hadn't taken time to put on Sunny's harness. Teddy remained behind them, watching.

Now Lyss and Gabe were coming toward them. Jennifer held her breath. Gabe was smiling . . . that was good. No, Gabe wasn't smiling. Gabe was *beaming*. His face was positively *glowing* with happiness and pride.

Lyss was smiling, too, looking from Daniel to Jennifer. Then she stopped walking and started running. Gabe, too, stopped, but he remained where he was, unmoving, smiling that same, wonderful smile as he watched his wife and a sobbing Jennifer fall into each other's arms just before Daniel cut in and gave Lyss a big brother bear hug.

"You're as beautiful as ever!" Jennifer choked out between tears. "More beautiful! Oh, Lyss—you look wonderful!"

Gabe came up behind Lyss and stood watching. He smiled with delight as Lyss and Jennifer continued to embrace and cry and laugh and say foolish things to one another.

"Do I still look like myself to you?" Lyss questioned seriously when the two of them had managed to recover a modicum of control.

"You *do;* you really *do!*" Jennifer stood back, holding her sister-in-law at arm's length to study her more carefully.

"Most of the scars around my hairline will fade. And the stitch marks, too," Lyss explained without self-consciousness. "It'll never be perfect, but—"

"—but then it never was," Daniel drawled, offering the expected older brother wisecrack, smiling when Lyss punched him playfully in the rib cage.

"Aren't you going to look at me, Daniel?" she asked, her expression sobering somewhat as she took her brother's hands and placed them on either side of her face.

"You bet I am," he said with a wobbly grin. "We need an objective opinion on all this."

His fingertips went over her face in light, deft movements, lingering on the scars as if he longed to heal them. "Well, Pip," he said lightly, his voice none too steady as he completed his inspection, "it seems to me that you're lookin' good. Real good." He paused. "There's just one thing, though . . . "

"What, Daniel?"

His index finger lightly traced her nose. He frowned, saying nothing.

Lyss giggled. "I finally got rid of the Kaine nose. I told you I was going to get a nose job some day."

"What's so terrible about the Kaine nose?" he said with a wounded look.

"On you, it looks good, Daniel," Lyss said, a smile spilling over in her voice. "On me, it just looked . . . big."

His eyes narrowed.

"Don't fret, Daniel," Jennifer told him. "I've always liked your nose. It gives your face a great deal of strength."

"A *great* deal," Gabe said gleefully.

Before Daniel could retaliate, Jason came running up with the Angelini children and Teddy. Lyss hugged everyone, including a suddenly shy Teddy.

"Gabe, would you get that package out of the trunk for me, please?" Lyss asked, turning to her husband.

"That's the *real* reason I wanted to come today," she explained as Gabe went back to the car. Her gaze went to Stacey, who was staring up at Lyss with solemn, awe-filled eyes.

"We had a very special delivery to make," Lyss went on. "I was told that today is someone's birthday." She smiled at Stacey, who bobbed her head up and down excitedly.

Gabe returned with the package and handed it to his wife. Lyss in turn placed the long, brightly wrapped box in the little girl's arms, saying, "This is for you, Stacey." She paused, then added softly, "Just for you. With my love."

With dancing eyes, Stacey squealed, then dropped down on the ground to open the gift. Her mouth blew out an excited "Oohhh!" as she carefully lifted from the wrappings a brand new, curly maple fiddle with its bow.

She studied it lovingly for a long moment before turning her gaze on Lyss and then Gabe. "My *own* fiddle?"

It was Gabe who answered. "Truly your own, dumpling. Lyss made it for you."

"I've never made a fiddle before, Stacey. Only dulcimers. I hope it's a good one."

Holding the fiddle to her heart as if it were a rare and precious treasure, the little girl looked up from her Indian-style perch and said with great dignity, "It's the most perfect fiddle in the world. It's even more better than Gabe's."

Gabe smiled, and after a moment, dug down in his pants pocket to pull out a small package, wrapped in plain brown paper. He looked at Nicky, then handed him the package.

"Nicky? I know it's not your birthday," he said quietly, "but I asked Lyss to make something for you, too. Something . . . special." He looked the boy squarely in the eye and added, "After all, you're an adopted member of our family now."

Wide-eyed, Nicky hesitated, then took the package. "May I open it now, Mr. Denton?" he asked, obviously trying to restrain his enthusiasm.

"Please do," Gabe said dryly.

Jennifer knew her brother-in-law well enough to know he

was suppressing a smile. Curious, she watched as Nicky slowly and methodically removed the wrapping and opened the lid of a small, delicately carved wooden box.

The boy caught a sharp breath. He looked up at Gabe with disbelief for a long time before returning his gaze to the box in his hand. With great care, he lifted from the box an exquisitely carved wooden replica of a golden retriever. The figurine looked exactly like Sunny.

After clearing his throat awkwardly, Gabe asked, "Did you see the inscription on the box lid?"

Nicky looked at him, glanced down at the box, then read aloud in a faltering voice:

"For Nicky Angelini: Because I owe him." Nicky swallowed hard before adding in a voice so soft Jennifer had to strain to hear, "It's signed . . . *'Gabe.'* "

The entire group was silent as Nicky stared up into Gabe's eyes with a stunned, overwhelmed expression. After a long moment, he finally offered his hand to Gabe, his expression sober as he said, with obvious difficulty, "I—I don't know what to say, sir."

Gabe looked at him. "How about . . . 'thank you, Gabe'. " A corner of his mouth quirked. Then he grinned and took Nicky's hand. "Please? I'm really tired of being called 'sir'. "

Jennifer held her breath as she watched, knowing how difficult this was for both of them.

Nicky stared at Gabe for another few seconds. Suddenly, in what Jennifer was certain must have been the first impulsive gesture of this strange little man-child's life, the boy moved in and hugged Gabe tightly around the waist. Gabe's face creased with pleasure as he wrapped Nicky snugly in his arms, releasing him only when Lyss put her arms around both of them.

"Hey! How about a hug for the whittler?"

Laughing, Nicky threw his arms around her and thanked her. Not about to be left out of this communal display of affection, Stacey jumped up and joined her brother in Lyss's arms.

Jennifer watched, wondering what he was up to when she saw Gabe stoop and whisper something to the Angelini children. They turned, glanced over at her and Daniel and came to them, carrying their gifts.

Stacey looked up at Daniel, then very carefully took one of his large hands and placed it on her precious new fiddle. "Here, Uncle Dan—do you want to look at my fiddle?"

"And my retriever, too," Nicky added, smiling at Jennifer.

His expression sober, Daniel took the fiddle and went over it gently with his hands. Shifting it under one arm, he then took the small wooden figurine from Nicky and examined it.

"These are absolutely beautiful," he said seriously, as he returned the children's treasures. "But I'm not surprised. Anything Lyss touches becomes a work of art."

He stopped, a fleeting look of mischief scurrying across his features when he heard Gabe cough. "Well," he said with a smile, "*almost* anything."